OH, SO YOU'RE STICKING AROUND, THEN.

THAT'S GOOD. IF YOU'D BEEN TEN SECONDS EARLIER, YOU WOULD HAVE FOUND YOURSELF LOOKING AT MY BARE BOTTOM.

NOT THAT THERE'S ANYTHING WRONG WITH MY BOTTOM.

IT'S QUITE CUTE ACTUALLY.

funny
kid

funn

written and illustrated
by Matt Stanton

For Chren.

Thank you for being
Max's great champion and
for getting in the trenches with us.

Onward and upward!

1 Every hero has an origin story ...

Can you remember being born?

I can. I know I was a baby at the time, but I've got a really good memory.

There I was, all cozy and warm, watching TV. (If you're feeling confused, yes, there was a TV in my mom's tummy. There was probably one in your mom's too, you just don't remember.)

I was watching *Captain Kickbutt*, which is still the most awesome cartoon on TV, when suddenly there was this creaking sound.

It's probably nothing, I told myself. Just something wrong with the plumbing again. I went back to my show. Then the walls began to

wobble! To be honest, I thought we were having an earthquake.

Now, you have to understand, these were the walls of my happy place. I'd spent a good nine months decorating! I'd hung up pictures, there was a mirror so that I had someone to talk to, even an inspirational quote or two on the fridge.

Then I heard someone say, "Looks like we're having a baby!" Weird. I wanted to yell:

But then things
really started to move.
I'll spare you the details, but try
to imagine ... actually, don't.
Just don't.
Finally it was over, and
FLASH-BUMP-BOING
I was out and everyone could
see my bum.

The doctor gave me to my mom and dad, and they said things like, "It's a boy" and "I can't believe he's real" and "His face looks a bit funny." Yeah, well, I'd like to see your face after doing the obstacle course I just did. Cut me some slack, people!

Instead they cut the umbilical cord, took me home, and called me Max.

* * * *

Even back then I was a funny kid.

I quickly discovered that no one had been entertaining my parents, so I figured that must be why they'd brought me on board.

My mom is a boss in a big company and my dad invents strange things in our backyard shed. They're pretty busy, so I run the house. I make sure the meals get eaten, the clothes get dirtied, and the rooms get messed up so that there's always something to clean at the end of the day. To be honest, I think my parents were a little lost before I came along.

It's up to me to ask them questions they can't answer. For example:

It helps them stay mentally sharp.

After they've had a long and difficult day, I like to help them put their feet up, prop pillows behind their heads, and play the what-are-we-doing-tomorrow? game. It goes like this:

THE WHAT-ARE-WE-DOING-TOMORROW? GAME

You can play for hours. They love it. It helps them relax at the end of the day and I know that because the game nearly always ends with a conversation about going to bed.

And you know what? When Mom makes me hug her good night, I'm sure I can still hear the *Captain Kickbutt* theme song playing on repeat inside her tummy.

I always get in trouble for leaving the TV on.

A few years after I was born, Mom and Dad had another baby, my little sister, Rosie. That was probably a mistake though.

They didn't realize they'd won the lottery with me, even though I tried to tell them having a kid with my level of awesome was pretty rare. Lightning doesn't strike in the same place twice, people! I was a blessing. Rosie's a dingbat.

I take my job as Chief Walburt Entertainer (CWE) very seriously, although not everyone appreciates it. I dressed up as a clown once to try to make my grandpa laugh. For some reason, he *really* didn't like that. He told me the only use for clowns was as food for the circus lions. Then he went and sat on the toilet for the rest of our visit.

My grandpa is a grump. Mom says he thinks Planet Earth is his house and everyone else popped in without asking. Dad says not to worry about it and just to pretend that Grandpa has that look on his face because you interrupted him sucking on a lemon.

I tried sucking on a lemon. It *does* do that to your face!

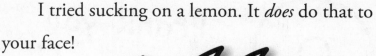

But I don't let party poopers like Grandpa stop me. Making people laugh is the best thing ever. It's also pretty much the only thing I'm good at. Being the funny kid is a good gig and I'll get Grandpa to smile one day. I know I will.

That is, if the police can ever find him.

2 Prank you very much!

I'm getting way ahead of myself. Let's go back to Tuesday – the day Grandpa goes missing.

It starts like any other Tuesday – with me trying to play a prank on our new teacher. (Who am I kidding? I try to play a prank on our new teacher every day. It's important to practice these things!)

MAX? WHAT DO YOU HAVE IN YOUR POCKET?

That's Miss Sweet. Miss Sweet has just started teaching our class at Redhill Middle School after our last teacher … well, you know how it goes. If you can't take the heat, get out of the … out of the … fireplace?

"Nothing!" I reply. This is a lie, of course, but not a bad one. It's a setup. I don't *want* her to believe me. I don't want anyone else to believe me either.

I want everybody's attention though, and now I have it.

I continue to fumble in my pocket. We're all sitting at our desks, trying to work on math problems or something, but now all the kids in my class are wondering what I'm hiding.

PSSST. WHAT ARE YOU DOING?

That's Hugo.

I'm Hugo's best friend, but I'm leaving *my* best friend position vacant. You never know who might come along. In the meantime though, ol' Hugo's more than welcome to hang around.

Hugo wants to know the gag, but can wait like everyone else. You can't ask me what happens at the end of the movie when it's only just started!

WAIT FOR IT. THIS IS GOING TO BE GOOD.

Miss Sweet is walking toward my desk and straight into my trap. She's very young for a teacher. Apparently this is her first job after college, which is both good and bad. Good because it makes her the ideal candidate for pranks – her teacher senses aren't tuned yet to the dangers of the class clown. Bad because it takes time to figure out a new teacher and this one is extra puzzling.

Miss Sweet doesn't yell, she doesn't throw pens, she never stands on chairs and points at you. Miss Sweet has this superpower where everyone desperately wants to be liked by her, so kids just do what she wants without her needing to yell at them. It's really weird. Plus, it makes the whole Student versus Teacher battle much trickier when the teacher is … nice.

"Stand up, please, young Max."

"I don't think this is a good idea, Max," Hugo hisses as I stand up. "Whatever your idea is."

Miss Sweet stops in front of me. "Take your hand out of your pocket," she says.

I MUST ADVISE AGAINST THAT, MISS SWEET.

"That's okay, Max," she says, and smiles. Smiles! Who is this teacher? "You don't need to advise me. You can just do what I ask you to do, thank you."

Everyone in class is watching. Out of the corner of my eye, I can see Kevin and Layla and Abby ... ugh, Abby. We'll get to her later. For now, just imagine chomping on a pickle that's covered in mustard and frog vomit. Yep. Abby makes life taste like that.

All the kids are craning their necks, trying to see what I'm going to take out of my pocket. This is working perfectly. It's no good being funny by yourself. (Well, it is, but if anyone sees you telling yourself jokes and then laughing hysterically, they'll send you to a special doctor.)

A funny kid needs an audience, which means you have to get everyone's attention first. I find using a little suspense is a great way to get it.

Slowly I remove my hand from my pocket. I keep it in a closed fist. The thing everyone wants to see is hidden inside my fingers.

Miss Sweet extends her open hand toward me. "Give it to me, please," she says.

I love this moment ... right before everyone bursts into laughter. I can sense the love and adoration I'm about to receive. I can almost touch it.

I stretch out my fist … uncurl my fingers … and give Miss Sweet a live mouse!

She shrieks!

The mouse squeaks!

Miss Sweet flicks away her hand.

...ouse flies ... e air and ...ugo's hair!

...Hugo screams.

He leaps up and the mouse goes flying again, this time straight onto Layla's nose with a squelch and a squeak.

Layla makes a sound that reminds me of an elephant sitting on a hedgehog, and the mouse drops, scampers across the floor, and up Ryan's leg into his shorts! It must be warm and cozy in there.

Ryan stands bolt upright, knocks over two desks, and then flees out the classroom door, the poor little mouse clinging to his undies and creating a strange-looking lump on Ryan's bottom.

SQUEEEAAAKKK!

A room full of furious eyes glare at me.

"MAAAAX!" they all yell at once.

Really? Not one laugh?

Miss Sweet looks at me. Even after that, she won't yell. How is that even possible? What does a kid have to do?

"I think you just earned yourself a lunchtime detention, funny kid," she says.

Abby Purcell decides this is a good time for her to speak up.

MORE LIKE THE UN-FUNNY KID!

Oh. So people laugh at that?

3

Okay, I probably need a plan to deal with this ...

"The Unfunny Kid. The UNFUNNY KID?"

Hugo, Duck, and I are walking from school to the auditions for the Redhill talent quest. It's called Redhill's Got Talent or something.

I guess I should be focusing on my audition, but I can't get today's comedy disaster out of my head.

The Unfunny Kid! That nickname better not stick.

"It could have been worse," Hugo says as we make our way down the main street of Redhill, heading toward the town hall, where the auditions are being held.

HOW COULD IT HAVE BEEN WORSE, HUGO? I MADE A JOKE AND NO ONE LAUGHED. THAT'S THE DEFINITION OF WORST. THEN ABBY PURCELL MADE A JOKE AND PEOPLE DID LAUGH. THAT'S THE DEFINITION OF WORST-EST. OR SHOULD BE. IF WORST-EST WAS A WORD. WHICH IT ISN'T.

"You could have been sent to the principal," Hugo says. "I thought that was going to happen for sure. Hey, where did you even get the mouse from?"

"Duck caught it for me," I reply. Duck looks up when he hears his name. My devoted feathered friend follows me everywhere. I tell everyone it's because I've trained him. The truth is, he thinks I'm his mommy ... but I keep that to myself for obvious reasons.

"Miss Sweet is lovely," Hugo says with a blissful smile on his face. Ugh, yuck.

"She can't be lovely, Hugo. If she's lovely, then everyone will love her. And if everyone loves her, then I can't play pranks on her."

"Everyone *does* love her."

"Exactly," I say. 'The worst-est.'"

The town hall is in front of us now, and hanging outside is a big banner advertising the talent quest this Saturday. It's to raise money for Redhill Nursing Home. That's where Grandpa lives.

One way to make everyone forget today's comedy catastrophe is for me to win the talent quest with my stand-up comedy routine.

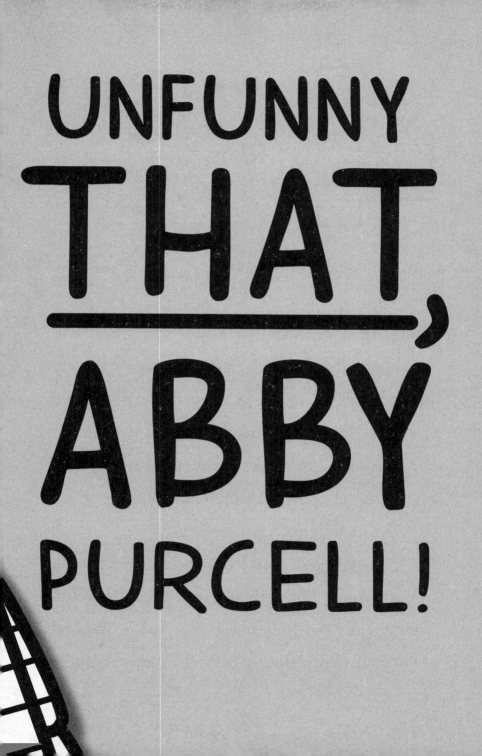

4

Nothing funny about a farting clown!
(Don't laugh!)

All the contestants are taken backstage by the stage manager, a skinny guy named Rupert. His pants are so tight they look like they've been stuck onto his legs, like the way Dad puts plastic on my schoolbooks. I wonder if Rupert has to squeeze out the air bubbles when he puts his pants on in the morning. He makes us stand in a big semicircle. I end up next to Abby Purcell.

"Oh, hi there, Unfunny Kid!"

Imagine that your shadow could talk to you. All the time. About the most boring things. On and on and on. Well, that's what Abby's like, and wherever I go, she manages to be there too.

I'M SURE YOU'RE ALL FEELING PRETTY NERVOUS.

Rupert rubs his hands together in circles like he's rolling a snot ball. I should tell Hugo. Hugo's a snot-rolling master.

Despite what our stage manager says, I'm not nervous at all.

"Performing in front of people is one of our species' biggest fears," he continues.

Not mine. The stage is my natural habitat. I was born for this. I've been making people laugh since day one. Unleash me on the world! Hollywood awaits!

"We are going to commence with some relaxation exercises."

This Rupert guy is taking it all very seriously. I can't believe he called us "species." Speak for yourself, pal.

Then someone farts.

"Sorry, that was me."

No, not me!

I turn to look at the contestant who claimed the gaseous eruption. It's a clown!

YOU SAID RELAXATION EXERCISES AND NOTHING HELPS ME RELAX MORE THAN LETTING A HAMSTER OUT OF THE HUTCH, IF YOU KNOW WHAT I MEAN?

People laugh at that. Not Rupert.

"What is your name, clown?"

"Me? Oh, I'm Tumbles."

"Well, Tumbles, I'd like to remind you that you're in the theater." Rupert says that last word like it's two words – the-ater. "A little respect, please."

"Yes, sir!" Tumbles salutes with his big red glove.

Rupert looks like he's got a hamster or two of his own, only his are stuck right up inside.

We do breathing exercises to de-stress, although no one seems more stressed than Rupert himself.

"Deep breath in. Hold. Hold. Okay, breathe out. Slowly. Slowly. Tumbles! No raspberries!"

There are only two people who aren't finding Tumbles very funny.

Rupert, because I think he accidentally got a whole roll of toilet paper stuck in his bottom last

time he went to the bathroom, and me, because I was not expecting to be competing with another comedian.

I look around at the other contestants. They are more like what I had in mind. An opera singer, a man who has strapped a whole lot of saucepans to his body and is going to play Mozart on them, Abby Purcell pretending to be a magician, a mime artist, someone with a puppet, and a guy dressed as a horse.

In other words, I was expecting a whole stage full of pathetic performances that make the

audience feel like they have indigestion for an hour.

Then I would come on as the funny kid, everyone would laugh, and I would win the competition and sign a ten-million-dollar book deal.

Only now we have a problem. Someone else is funny.

I think I'd better go talk to him.

I don't have to wait long for my opportunity. Rupert explains how the auditions are going to work – there are three judges who will decide if we make the cut to perform for the whole town on Saturday – then he puts us in a line. Tumbles and I find ourselves at the end behind Abby. I turn around to face him, comic versus comic.

"Just so you know, Tumble-Pants, you're going down." I point at the puffy flowers that are stuck to his clown suit as I talk.

"Really? And who's going to beat me? You?" The clown folds his enormous arms.

I DON'T NEED TO PUT ON MAKEUP TO BE FUNNY.

Ooh, good one, Max (if I do say so myself).

Tumbles draws an invisible circle around my face with his finger.

IF YOU DID THOUGH, IT WOULD HELP DEAL WITH ALL OF THAT UGLY.

Abby bursts out laughing.

Grrrrrrr …

All right, Tumbles.
You're going to pay
for that.

5 I cannot work under these conditions!

Most of the other contestants audition and they're as terrible as you'd expect. I've got this sewn up.

Then it's Abby Purcell's turn.

Sonic the Hedgehog has Dr. Robotnik. Ben 10 has Vilgax. I have Abby Purcell.

She thinks she's going to beat me with a few magic tricks. Abby walks onto the stage wearing a black cape and a top hat. The hall is silent. Tumbles and I watch from the wings.

"Good afternoon, ladies and gentlemen," she begins. "I am Abby the Purcellian, magician extraordinaire. I am an illustrator of illusion,

a heroic hypnotist, and a master of mystery.
And, what's more, I'm only eleven!"

Oh, give me a break.

Abby lifts her top hat to reveal a white bunny
perched on her head.

Big deal.

> IT'S NO GREAT TRICK
> TO HIDE A RABBIT UNDER
> YOUR HAT ...

I agree.

"... but it's quite something
to hide a cat under your rabbit."
As she lifts the bunny off her
head, she reveals a kitten hiding underneath it.
The judges clap.

Tumbles whispers into my ear like a devil on
my shoulder. "Ooh, she's good."

"Go back to the circus, Dumbo!" I hiss.

Abby
proceeds to juggle
the hat, rabbit, and cat.
Surely they can't be real.
How is she even doing that?
She then holds out the hat, and the
rabbit and the cat fall inside it.
I'm having a bit of a hard
time pretending to be
unimpressed.

Then she shows everyone the inside of the hat and it's completely empty!

I peek around the curtains as Abby takes a bow. The judges are giving her a standing ovation!

And for the very first time, I feel nervous. My jokes are funny, right? Quick, I need to do some of Rupert's relaxation exercises, but as soon as I close my eyes, I think of Tumbles farting, and that's the last thing I need.

"Next! Max Walburt!"

Okay, pull it together, Max. Time to bring the comedy gold. I clench my fists and wiggle my toes. I'm pumped. Let's do this.

LET'S SEE WHAT YOU'VE GOT, MAX.

I turn to Tumbles. "It won't be hard to be funnier than a clown."

"We'll see," he says with a big grin on his face. Then again, he always has a big grin on his face. It's painted on.

I don't care. I'm focused. This is my moment. Nothing can throw me off my game.

I walk out into the middle of the stage … and the clown boos me!

I can't believe it! Did he really just do that? I glare back at the wings.

BOO! YOUR JOKES SMELL LIKE MY DOG'S ARMPITS!

That's not even funny. Dogs don't even have armpits!

I turn back to face the judges and see that they're trying really hard not to laugh. That would be fine, except they're not finding me funny! They're laughing at the stupid clown who's heckling me!

"Try facing the other way! I bet your bum tells better jokes than your face!" Tumbles yells out.

Grrrr! Does anyone have a hose?

On the stage in front of me is a clock. It's already counting down my time! My mind has gone completely blank. I can't even remember my first joke!

I only have three more minutes to impress the judges and this clown is completely putting me off.

"Wake me up when this chump's finished and the actual funny kid arrives!"

I turn toward the wings and give the fiercest death stare I can, but I can't even see the clown.

He's hiding back in the shadows somewhere. Then he has the nerve to start snoring like a retired hippopotamus!

I look out at the three judges for help. Come on, guys!

One of them is knitting. I don't think she's glanced up once. The next one is on his phone. He appears to be taking selfies. The third one is laughing hysterically – at the clown!

SNOOOOORE!

Two and a half minutes.

"Pssst. Just start! Ignore him!"

That's Hugo from the front row. I can't even think properly! Is this what they mean by stage fright? I'm paralyzed.

SNOOOOOOOORE!

The lights onstage are trying to melt me. I can feel sweat running from the back of my neck all the way down to my bottom.

Hugo's right. I just need to begin.

Two minutes.

"Breakfast is the most important meal of the day," I say into the microphone. Pause for the punch line. "So I like to save it until last."

Hugo falls off his chair in hysterics.

Okay, don't overdo it, buddy.

He's fogging up his glasses and slapping his tummy until it wobbles. I keep going.

"Are they like, 'Hey, Jerry? What cologne are you wearing?'" Pause, this time because I need to try to pronounce the next bit properly. "'Is that Putrid du Jour?'"

Not even Hugo laughs at that one. My French accent probably needs some work.

There aren't that many people in the hall, thank goodness. Mostly just the other contestants and a few of their friends.

I can hear Hugo explaining my first joke to the person next to him. "Because if you move it to the last meal, then it won't really be breakfast anymore. See? Wait, did he just do the skunk one? Did I miss the skunk one?"

Less than a minute to go.

If I don't make these judges laugh, they won't even let me into the talent quest. My reputation as a funny kid will be shot if I'm not even good enough to compete!

And if I'm not the funny kid, what am I? Just … Max? Ugh.

One last crack. I decide to go with a knock-knock joke and end on a high note. Let's hope the judges play ball.

"Knock, knock."

"Come in!" yells the clown from the wings.

The judges were supposed to answer! I do not want to do this joke with a clown.

I look desperately at the judges. For the first time in my whole comedy set, they actually look interested. The granny has even stopped knitting. I try again.

KNOCK, KNOCK.

THE DOOR'S OPEN, KIDDO. JUST COME IN!

The judges laugh. I look down at Hugo. He raises his eyebrows as if to say, "What have you got to lose? They are laughing, aren't they?"

Okay, fine.

I turn and glare at the curtains.

> I SAY, "KNOCK, KNOCK."
> YOU SAY, "WHO'S THERE?"

Do I really have to spell it out?

> BUT WHY?
> THE DOOR'S ALREADY OPEN.

Apparently I do.

> JUST SAY,
> **"WHO'S THERE?"**

"Jeepers! Calm down, squirt. Okay, fine. Who's there?"

Thank you. Was that too much to ask?

"Goanna," I say.

"What's a goanna?"

Grrrr …

"Ooh, ooh, I know!" It's Hugo, almost jumping out of his pants. This is not supposed to be a quiz show! "It's a type of lizard!"

"Why is there a lizard knocking on my door?" Tumbles calls out.

"Just play along, would you?" I plead.

"All right. All right," says the clown, seeming to give in. "Come in, lizard!"

"NOT COME IN! You have to ask me my last name!" I yell.

"A lizard with a last name? I've never met a lizard with a last name."

The judges might be laughing, but I want to

go find that clown, rip that red nose right off his face, and splat a tomato there instead.

Do not lose your cool, Max. I grit my teeth. Hold it together.

JUST PRETEND. PLEASE?

"Oh, okay. I get it," replies the clown. "What's your last name, lizard?"

"You say, 'GOANNA WHO?' Why can't you just say, 'GOANNA WHO?' How have you never EVER heard of a knock-knock joke?"

There goes my cool. Guess it's well and truly lost now.

"This is supposed to be a joke?"

BUZZZZZZZ!

And my time is up.

I stand there in the center of the stage, trembling with rage, waiting for the judges to pull themselves together and stop laughing ... at the flipping clown!

I look down at Hugo. He shrugs and gives me a thumbs-up, as if to say, "Yes, that was an absolute disaster and you were upstaged by someone who wasn't even on the stage, but at least you're not ... well ... dead or something?"

Thanks, buddy.

The judges do some whispering among themselves.

I catch Abby Purcell's eye. She mouths, "The Unfunny Kid," and grins. I wish I could make her disappear into her stupid magic hat.

"Ah, Max?" It's one of the judges.

"Yes?"

"We're going to let you through, because that was very funny, even if the funny bits weren't really … well … you."

That felt like nonsense mixed in with an insult and offered as a compliment.

"So, I'm through?" I ask.

The granny judge clears her throat. "We feel sorry for you. You can have another turn on Saturday, love," she says, and goes back to her knitting.

Hugo claps.

I turn and get ready to thump a clown.

What's a hero without a superpower?

(Batman ... Iron Man ... Mickey Mouse ...)

Tumbles must sense I'm coming to give him the biggest wedgie of his life, because he runs out onto the stage before I've even come off.

"Is it my turn yet? Is it my turn?" he calls to the judges.

I glance over at the three of them. I can't very well bash up a circus clown on the stage of the town hall, can I?

"We saved the best till last!" replies the selfie judge.

I turn to Tumbles as he walks to the microphone. "Two can play at this game."

He grins. "Go for it, Max. Give as good as

you got. In the meantime, have one of my flowers, poppet."

He thrusts a yellow plastic flower into my hand as I climb down the steps. I sit next to Hugo in the front row and give him the flower.

I DON'T WANT THIS JUNK.
YOU CAN HAVE IT.

Oh, boy, am I going to ruin this clown's act.

Tumbles stands in the center of the stage, looking out at the lights and the judges.

"Did Mommy do your makeup for you?" I call out. He ignores me. He doesn't even blink. Wow, that's impressive. It's like I'm not even here. He begins his act.

YOU KNOW WHEN YOU'RE IN A PUBLIC TOILET AND YOU'RE DOING A POOP ...

Hugo chuckles, looking fondly at the plastic flower. I glare at him.

"You can't laugh, Hugo!" I whisper.

"But what if –?"

"Nope! That's exactly what he wants," I say. "Whatever he does, you cannot laugh. It's a matter of willpower, Hugo. Willpower!"

Hugo nods. Then he shakes his head. Then he looks confused. "I'm not sure I have any of that."

Tumbles continues.

THERE YOU ARE, SITTING IN YOUR STALL,
MINDING YOUR OWN BUSINESS ...
OR SHOULD I SAY,
DOING YOUR OWN BUSINESS ...

The judges laugh. I turn quickly and stare at Hugo. He's not blinking and his lips are pressed tightly together, like he's trying to hold in a sneeze.

"Don't do it, Hugo," I warn him.

"… and suddenly you realize that there's a second plopper," Tumbles says. More chuckling.

Time for another heckle. I stand up and yell:

YOU'RE A NINCOMPOOP
WHO CAN'T POOP!

Well, that killed the laughing. There's complete silence now.

I nudge Hugo. "You can laugh at that!"

Now he looks really confused. "What? Which bit can I laugh at?"

"My bit!"

"What did you say?"

Grrrr …

Tumbles continues as though nothing happened. How does he do that? This clown is some sort of professional.

YOU KNOW WHICH PLOPS ARE YOURS, OR AT LEAST YOU THINK YOU DO. BUT YOU WONDER ABOUT THE PLOPPING IN THE STALL NEXT DOOR. DO YOU EVER ASK YOURSELF WHO IS DOING THE PLOPPING? WHO IS THE SECOND PLOPPER?

There's a murmur of understanding in the hall.

"Like, maybe it's the queen," says Tumbles. "How would the queen poop?"

The judges start to really laugh as Tumbles purses his big clown lips and makes high-pitched, posh plopping sounds.

"They'd be awfully polite plops, I suspect," he says. "Or maybe it's a sumo wrestler?"

I look at Hugo. His face has turned a light shade of blue, his lips are glued shut, and there are tears rolling out from under his glasses. He's trying very hard not to laugh.

"I've always imagined a sumo wrestler's poop sounds a bit like a tsunami. There's a warning siren and people are just running for their lives. Head for the hills!"

One of the male judges falls off his chair. The granny judge is using her knitting to wipe the tears of laughter from her face.

This is bad. Really bad. Tumbles is killing it. Why isn't my heckling having any effect? I stand up and deliver a poem I've been working on.

"Turn that clown upside down! Change his smile to a frown! Poops his pants till they're brown!"

Okay, so it's not Shakespeare, but it's pretty good, right?

It's like I dropped a wet towel on the whole room. *Thud.* Everyone looks at me, including the judges, but not a single person laughs. Instead they look annoyed.

Finally the selfie judge speaks. "Max. If you don't stop interrupting, we're going to have to ask you to leave."

"What? That blasted clown interrupted my whole act!"

No one seems to see the logic of this. I just get more fierce eyes staring at me.

Slowly I sit back down. I don't understand. I had one superpower. One thing I could do well. I was the funny kid. I could make everyone laugh. But I've lost it. It's gone. In the space of a single day, I can no longer do my one thing!

I tell you what, if having people laugh at your jokes is the best feeling in the world, having people not laugh at them is the worst.

I don't hear the rest of Tumbles's act. Everyone laughs at it though. Hugo pats me on the shoulder as if to say, "I'm starting an I-suck-at-life club and you'd be very welcome." I just stare at my shoes.

Maybe I'm done. I should just never try to tell a joke again. Maybe there's something else I'm good at? I've never tried quilting. Perhaps I'll try to make an awesome quilt.

While the judges are telling Tumbles that he's going to win the talent quest for sure and they can't wait to see him perform, I turn to Hugo.

7

Don't look at the other page! There's a turtle bottom.

"Sounds like you lost your mojo," says Mom.

Hugo is staying over at our house, because his parents are overseas for a week. We're sitting at the dinner table, eating a pie Dad made. He called it a Humble Pie or something, but I think he was just trying to be funny.

Dad's a pretty good cook, although my little sister, Rosie, doesn't think so. She is munching on a plastic car instead. "Yum, yum, yum."

"What's a mojo?" Hugo asks.

"My dignity. My pride. My reason for living," I answer. I actually don't know what mojo means. I don't care either. To say I'm feeling grumpy would be like saying a bear who has been asleep for the whole of winter is feeling a tad peckish. I'm as glum as a homeless turtle.

I'M COLD AND EVERYONE'S LOOKIN' AT MY BUTT.

"No, no," Mom says. "Mojo is like your magic."

"Like when a golfer goes off their game or a writer gets writer's block or Beyoncé comes down with laryngitis," Dad says. Dad loves Beyoncé. There's nothing more embarrassing than walking around the mall while your father hums "Single Ladies." He even throws in a few of the dance moves for a little extra humiliation.

"Maybe Max needs a life coach?" Hugo suggests.

"I don't need a life coach. I need a box with a lid on it that I can go and sit in. Forever."

"Yep. You definitely need a life coach," Hugo continues. "My uncle had a life coach once who helped him quit his job as a garbage collector and become a singer. He's not a very good singer though."

"Just a small box," I say. "I don't want it to be in anybody's way."

"Rosie, eat some of your pie," Dad says,

pulling the car out of her mouth. "Hugo, you might need to be Max's life coach."

Now that is a terrible idea.

"How do I do that?" Hugo asks.

"Forget it, Hugo. I'm fine," I say.

"You have to get him into a peak state for maximum performance," Dad explains. It seems he's been reading his motivational books again. He particularly likes one called *Awaken the Abominable Snowman Within.*

A PEAK STATE? WHAT'S A PEAK STATE? DO YOU MEAN PUT HIM IN THE EMPIRE STATE?

Rosie rejects the pie again and starts munching on her shoe.

"You can put me in *whatever* state for all I care," I say. "I'll still be the Unfunny Kid and I'm not competing in the talent quest."

A PEAK STATE IS WHEN YOU FEEL UNSTOPPABLE, LIKE YOU CAN DO ANYTHING. SO, HUGO, YOU COULD SAY THINGS LIKE, "IT'S NOT GETTING KNOCKED DOWN THAT MATTERS, IT'S HOW FAST YOU GET BACK UP" OR "GET BACK ON THE HORSE, MAX." YOU KNOW, ENCOURAGE HIM.

Hugo looks very confused. I'm not so sure he's getting this. Either way, I don't care. No amount of motivation is going to help me. I'm beyond help.

Hugo's going to try anyway.

"Um … be like a horse, Max."

Ugh.

The phone rings.

"That's not quite right, Hugo, but good try," Mom says.

Dad answers the phone.

"Yes, Dr. Duncanbray," Dad says. Then there is lots of "uh-huh" and "I see" and "that doesn't sound good" and "we'll come right over."

Then he hangs up. Rosie's flossing her two teeth with a shoelace.

"What's wrong?" Mom looks concerned.

"Grandpa's missing," Dad says. "It seems like he's gone off for a walk by himself and gotten lost."

"He's not supposed to leave the nursing home," Mom says. "It's not like him to just wander off."

"Maybe he lost his mojo too," I say.

"Okay, kids. We can't leave you here on your own. Everyone in the car," Dad says.

Hugo pats me on the arm.

COME ON, MAX. IT'S NOT HOW MANY TIMES YOU GET UP THAT MATTERS, YOU'LL STILL GET HIT IN THE FACE.

Not sure you've quite got the idea there, pal.

This chapter contains old people.

Redhill Nursing Home is where the old people in our town live. It's on a very quiet street on the other side of Redhill. Mom always says the nursing home is a pretty fun place, so I don't know why Grandpa would try to escape. They have board games and free food and TVs that stay on ALL THE TIME!

But when I look around the big room at all the old people sitting in chairs and staring into space, I realize Redhill Nursing Home is a lot like Redhill Middle School. For a start, everyone inside looks like they'd rather be somewhere else.

The old people are like schoolkids too. They

all seem to be talking too loudly, pulling funny faces, or daydreaming out the window. Whatever they're doing, they're not listening to the nurses.

The nurses are talking sweetly to the residents, like teachers do, but you can tell that some of them would rather drop-kick a few of the oldies up the bottom. But then they'd get fired and they probably need the paycheck, so that's probably the reason they don't.

Is that why Miss Sweet is being so nice to me? Because she needs the money?

We meet Dr. Duncanbray. He has too many teeth. They look very squashed in his mouth, like they were all trying to get out at the same time and got stuck.

He takes us to Grandpa's room.

HE CAME IN HERE TO HAVE A NAP AFTER LUNCH AND WE HAVEN'T SEEN HIM SINCE.

"Do you have security cameras?" Dad asks.

"Unfortunately they've been malfunctioning this afternoon," Dr. Duncanbray replies.

"That's bad timing," Mom says.

"There was a side door that was left open and we think he wandered out there for a walk."

DOES HE DO THAT OFTEN?

Dr. Duncanbray shakes his head.

I know I'm in a grumpy mood, but I must say I'm not too impressed with the outfit Dr. Duncanbray is running here. Open doors? Broken cameras? I mean, seriously, how can you lose an old man? It's not like Grandpa's going anywhere very quickly.

And it's this thought that makes me notice something.

I DIDN'T KNOW GRANDPA HAD A WALKING STICK.

I pick up a polished wooden cane from where it leans by the door.

"He doesn't," Dad says, and then looks at Dr. Duncanbray. "Does he?"

"Well, actually, we gave it to him this morning. We'd noticed he was getting a little slower on his feet, so we brought him the cane," replies the doctor. "He wasn't very happy about it. You know how he can be."

"What did he do?" Dad asks.

HE THREW IT AT ME.

"Maybe we should ask some of his friends if they know where he's gone?" Hugo suggests, looking back down the corridor toward the big room.

"Good idea," I reply, and walk out with Hugo. We pass a bulletin board that has a poster for the talent quest on it. Don't remind me!

YOUR GRANDPA DOESN'T REALLY HAVE ANY FRIENDS!

We ignore Dr. Duncanbray as he calls out after us. If you ask me, Dr. Duncanbray is cranky that Grandpa threw a walking stick at his head, so he's not trying very hard to find him.

It's time to get to the bottom of this ourselves. Hugo and I will take it from here.

The first person we talk to is a lady with cake in her mouth. I put on my polite voice.

EXCUSE ME, OLD LADY! MY GRANDPA LIVES IN THAT ROOM JUST DOWN THERE AND HE'S GONE MISSING! ARE YOU HIS FRIEND? DO YOU KNOW WHERE HE'S GONE?

ARE YOU CYRIL?

"What?"

"Cyril, is that you?" she asks again. Cake crumbs fly toward my face.

Hugo whispers in my ear, "I think she's asking if you like cereal."

"Yes, I do like cereal, but I'm looking for my grandpa." I speak slowly and loudly.

"And I'm looking for Cyril!" she yells suddenly, and I get a face full of sucked icing.

Yuck! We leap back and turn around.

Ahh! There's an old man folded in half and leaning on a walking frame right behind us.

"Are you Cyril?" Hugo asks him.

NO, NO, NO, YOUNG CHAPS. I'M SIR PHILLIP BARTHOLOMEW THE THIRD. CAN I ASSIST YOU?

Wonderful. Someone who's happy to help us.

"My grandpa lives in that room and he's gone for a walk. We're trying to find out if anyone knows where he went."

Sir Phillip Bartholomew the Third looks down at Grandpa's room and then back at us. He scratches his chin. "He's your grandpa, is he?"

"Yes!" I reply. This is great! He knows Grandpa!

"And he's gone off for a walk?"

Hugo and I nod.

"Fantastic," Sir Phillip Bartholomew the Third replies, and then a smile floods his face. "Hopefully he's been run over by a large horse!"

What?

The old man turns away from us and faces the rest of the big room.

ATTENTION, EVERYONE! WE HAVE SOME WONDERFUL NEWS! CRANKY-PANTS HAS RUN AWAY!

I don't believe it. An old lady starts cheering! A dude on the couch, who I honestly thought was dead, opens his eyes, stands up, and does a little dance!

"Who's Cranky-Pants?" I ask.

Suddenly another old lady (or is it an old man? I can't really tell with this one) has come out of nowhere.

PRAISE THE LORD, CRANKY-PANTS HAS GOTTEN LOST! JIGGITY, JIGGITY, JIGGITY!

Hugo and I look at each other.

"Are they having a party?" Hugo asks me. "I don't think I've ever seen old people this happy."

They certainly seem to be celebrating. Someone's turned on music and a lady with purple hair is attempting to climb up onto a table.

I turn around and see Mom, Dad, and Rosie

enter the big room with Dr. Duncanbray. The doctor quickly yells for one of the nurses to help him stop the old lady from table dancing.

YOU'RE GOING TO BREAK A HIP, GLADYS!

It seems I'm not the only person who doesn't really like Grandpa.

9

I spy with my little eye ... no Grandpa.

Mom and Dad take the three of us outside, because the nurses suddenly have their hands full being party poopers. Plus, it feels a little embarrassing being the family of the guy nobody likes!

It seems Grandpa has not been any friendlier to the people at his nursing home than he was to us.

I once asked Dad why Grandpa was always grumpy, and he said something about having a boring job his whole life, Grandma dying, and blah-blah-blah something about politics.

That seemed to make sense to Dad, but frankly none of it sounded like a good-enough reason for telling your grandson that milk might come from a cow's udder, but cheese comes from its butt. Or for the time Grandpa dressed up as Santa and told me the only present I was getting that year was something called the Plague.

I ALREADY GAVE IT TO THE REINDEER AND NOW THEY'RE ALL ... WELL, DEAD.

I glance up and down the street. The sun is setting now and it's starting to get dark. And cold. And boring.

"That's not what families do, Max," Dad says.

"Sure it is. He'd do the same for us," I say. "Or should I say he *wouldn't* do the same for us."

"You know, sometimes you really remind me of your grandpa, Max," Mom says.

"He could be anywhere by now," Hugo says as the streetlights click on.

"I'm going to call Debbie." Mom pulls out her phone. "She might be able to give us a hand. We want to find him before it gets too dark."

Mom steps away and starts talking into her phone, so I ask Dad, "Who's Debbie?"

"Mom's friend, the police officer," Dad explains, holding Rosie. "You know, Sergeant Purcell."

Hang on a minute. Purcell. *Purcell* ... Why does that sound familiar?

It's official. This is the most terrible day the universe ever invented.

You've got to be kidding me.

Sergeant Purcell is Abby Purcell's mom and it must be bring-your-kid-to-work day, because when Mom's friend arrives (not in her uniform, mind you ... how do we even know she's a real cop?) my archnemesis gets out of the car too.

I CAN'T DO THIS RIGHT NOW, ABBY. MY GRANDPA HAS GONE MISSING. HE COULD EVEN HAVE BEEN KIDNAPPED!

No one thinks he's been kidnapped.

MY MOM AND I WILL INVESTIGATE. SHE'S A COP.

"Yes, but just because *she's* a cop, that doesn't make *you* a cop."

"It pretty much does."

"Why is it called KIDnapped? Shouldn't it be OLDnapped?" Hugo asks.

"He might be *having* a nap," says Abby. "That's a good idea, Hugo. I'll pass it on to my sergeant."

SHE'S NOT YOUR SERGEANT! SHE'S YOUR MOM!

CHILL OUT, CUPCAKE.

"Max is a little stressed right now, Abby," says Hugo. "It's not the time to be calling each other names. We need to help Max."

Abby smirks. "Fair enough. What would you like me to do, Hugo?"

I've got an idea! Move to Pluto!

"Probably the best thing you could do," Hugo says, "is use your amazing magic skills to make Max's grandpa reappear."

What?

"She doesn't have any magic skills, Hugo!"

YES, SHE DOES! DID YOU SEE WHAT SHE DID WITH THE RABBIT AND THE CAT?

Abby's nodding. "It was pretty good, huh?"

"It was AMAZING!" Hugo says, his eyes wide. "You're totally going to win the talent quest."

Abby grins. I glare at him.

THAT MAKES SENSE. I MEAN, WHAT SORT OF ACT IS THE UNFUNNY KID GOING TO DO? YOU COULD READ OUT FUNERAL NOTICES? TELL US A STORY ABOUT PAINT DRYING? ACTUALLY, THAT MIGHT BE FUNNIER THAN YOUR JOKES ARE NOW.

Before I can strap both of them to a rocket launcher and shoot them into outer space, Abby's mom claps her hands to get our attention and take charge of the situation. Maybe she's been on a grandpa hunt before. I guess it's like an Easter egg hunt, except there's only one egg and it's not made of chocolate.

WE'LL DIVIDE INTO GROUPS AND WE'LL FAN OUT IN DIFFERENT DIRECTIONS. MAX AND HUGO, YOU HEAD DOWN THAT WAY. ABBY AND STEVE, YOU GO WITH THEM.

Steve? Who's Steve?

Abby disappears around the back of her car and returns with a giant dog on a leash. He's enormous! His nose is glistening wet, there's drool swinging from his mouth, and his tail is wagging so vigorously I'm sure it could send me flying down the street.

Did I mention that I hate dogs? For some reason, they're always obsessed with me. Maybe my natural odor is similar to dog biscuits?

Abby and the dog come bounding over. I hide behind Hugo.

"Keep that thing away from me!"

"Who? Steve?" Abby asks. "Steve's harmless. Unless you're a bad guy, then he's like a *T. rex* and he'll rip your head off. Are you a bad guy, Max?"

Gulp.

"He's so cuuuute!" Hugo says, tickling Steve under the chin.

"Yeah, cute like Godzilla," I say.

Steve stops smiling. He's staring at me. Apparently he didn't find that very funny.

Join the club, Steve! Join the club!

"Easy, Steve," Abby says, holding the leash. "Let's walk."

Once, when I was little, I was at the park

with Mom and Dad, eating ice cream. We bumped into our next-door neighbor and his dog. The grown-ups talked to each other and I guess I was supposed to talk to the dog. His name was Princess.

So, like a good kid, I politely asked Princess how he felt about the weather. Princess looked at me like I was crazy to be trying to talk to a dog and, instead of replying, ate my whole ice cream out of my hand in one giant gulp!

"Naughty dog, Princess!" I said.

But apparently that was the wrong thing to say, because our neighbor did that squat-to-talk-to-the-child thing and explained that we don't talk to Princess like that, as it makes him feel bad about himself.

Princess was feeling pretty pleased with himself, if you asked me. He had ice-cream drool all over his face. And sprinkles up his nose.

When I told everyone what happened, no one believed that the dog had stolen my ice cream, because, get this, our neighbor said that Princess doesn't eat dairy.

So I got in trouble and I lost my ice cream. As a result, I hate dogs. In my defense though, Princess started it.

Steve's still looking at me as we walk. I can see his shiny nose twitching.

"Abby? Get him to stop looking at me."

I dodge to the other side of Hugo, but Steve's gaze follows me. I scoot back the other way, but he follows me again.

"Steve, sit," Abby says confidently, but the dog completely ignores her. "He does seem interested in you, doesn't he? He must be able to smell fear."

"I'm not scared!" I say. Then Steve leaps around Hugo, straight at me. "*Aaarrrggghhh!*"

I bolt the other way and suddenly Steve is chasing me and we're running in circles around Hugo. Abby, of course, is connected to Steve by the leash, so now there are three of us running and screaming and barking, with Hugo getting spun around in the middle!

I'M IN A BLENDER!
I'M IN A BLENDER!
I'M IN A BLENDER!

I turn and run back up the street toward Sergeant Purcell's car and, somewhere, Mom and Dad. This is the only time running ever makes sense, when something is trying to eat you! I'm in such a panic I think I see Tumbles in a bush as I sprint past. All my nightmares at once!

Steve is hot on my tail, saliva flying and

warm canine breath blowing down the back of my neck like a super-stinky hair dryer.

Bump! Bump! Abby is being dragged along behind Steve, tumbling and tripping and yelling at full blast, "Stop, Max! Just let him eat you!"

"The car, Max!" Hugo calls.

Sure enough, Sergeant Purcell has left the back door of her car unlocked. I wrench it open and leap in. I don't have enough time to pull the door closed behind me. I crash and flip across the seat and smack my head into the opposite door.

Ugh.

To my surprise, Steve does not jump in behind me. Apparently he knows he's not allowed in the back seat of the car. Instead he sits calmly next to the door as though his job is done. Abby rolls to a stop beside him.

"Good dog, Steve. Good dog," she pants.

Good dog? What is it with dog people?

11

Disappearing old men and farting rockets are just the beginning ...

So it turns out Grandpa is quite the hiker. Either that or he has actually been kidnapped. After two hours of searching, no one can find him. Mom and Dad send Hugo and me home, because it's getting pretty late. Turns out the you-can't-stay-home-by-yourself rule doesn't apply now that things are a little more serious.

Hugo wants to stay up and watch puppies with Mohawks on YouTube, but I head straight to bed. It's the only way to make the worst day in the history of the universe end.

* * *

"Wake up! Max! Wake up!"

"Ugh. Hugo! Get off me! I only just fell asleep!" I try to thump him, but I haven't opened my eyes yet, so I end up punching myself in the ear.

"If I'm going to be your life coach, you've got to listen to me," Hugo says. "You've been sleeping all night, Max."

"No, I haven't. I've only been asleep for about three minutes," I reply, my eyes still shut. "And you're not my life coach! I had just started this dream about getting in a fart-powered rocket with Captain Kickbutt. It was going to be really awesome, but you ruined it!"

"Max, there are a whole lot of people with cameras on your front lawn!"

TIME FOR HYPER-DRIVE! QUICK! PULL THIS FINGER!

FART POWER

I open my eyes. What?

Hugo is over by the window, looking out through the curtains. He was right. It is morning. How did that happen? I climb out of bed and go see what he's looking at.

Sure enough, out in the street are some vans from Channel 11 and the local radio station, plus a whole bunch of other cars. Standing around them, including on our grass, are people with telephones and cameras.

"They look like reporters," I say.

"What are they doing here?"

"How would I know, Hugo? I've only just come back from piloting a farting rocket."

"We should probably go and wake up your parents," Hugo says.

"Waking Mom and Dad is always a bad idea. And they've been out all night looking for Grandpa. Have you seen how grumpy my dad gets first thing on a normal morning? He's like a toad with a toothache."

"But there are reporters on your front lawn."

"So? What's so scary about reporters?" I reply, heading toward the door. "Let's go talk to them."

Hugo grumbles something about no one ever listening to him or something. I'm too busy heading downstairs to catch it.

I open the front door and there is a flurry of activity outside. It's like the reporters are pigeons and I'm a leftover hamburger with no meat patty, sauce all licked off.

The problem is, I think these pigeons wanted a whole hamburger, not the leftovers, because as soon as they see it's me who opened the door, they stop.

"It's just a kid," a woman says.

"Hey, son, can you go get your parents for us?" a guy with a beard asks.

"What's with the duck?" says a dude in a hoodie who's leaning against our house, eating a hot dog. Is that your breakfast, man? That's weird.

I look down. Duck has hopped up next to me on the front step like he's my bodyguard. He's glaring at the pesky journalists and looking just as annoyed as me that no one said "good morning." He also seems a little bit interested in that guy's hot dog.

I AM NOT *JUST A KID!* I AM MAX WALBURT. I AM THE SPOKESPERSON FOR THIS FAMILY.

Hugo has appeared over my shoulder. "I really don't think this is a good idea," he whispers.

Shhh!

"Sorry, kid, but we can't interview you without your parents," says the guy with the beard.

"Why not? I'm eleven! I can tell you everything you need to know."

CAN WE INTERVIEW HIM OFF THE RECORD?

I DON'T THINK SO. WE'RE NOT ALLOWED TO ASK HIM QUESTIONS.

The woman looks very disappointed. I know how she feels. This is an opportunity to become famous for ... something. Doesn't really matter what, but it would be a shame to waste it.

Then I have an idea.

"I can ask questions though, right?" I ask.

The reporters look at each other and shrug. I don't think they'd thought of that.

"I'm pretty sure there aren't any rules about you asking us questions," beard guy says.

"Okay, good. I can work with that. You're here because you want to know about the talent quest, right?" I ask.

"The ... talent ... quest," the woman replies very slowly, moving her head around in a weird swirl as if she can't work out whether I'm speaking in code or not. I hear people complain about the state of journalism. This must be what they're talking about.

YES, THE REDHILL TALENT QUEST. I WAS GOING TO RELEASE A STATEMENT THIS MORNING.

"You were going to release a ... statement." I think she's decided that repeating what I say really slowly might work just as well as a question.

"You're interviewing him. You should stop," calls hot-dog guy.

Out of the corner of my eye, I see Duck's head snap around as if to say, "Shut it!" That's it, Duck. You deal with Mr. McWeird Breakfast over there.

"I'm not interviewing him," she replies. "He's just talking!"

I continue. "I was going to release a statement saying that I am quitting the talent quest."

"I can't … stop him talking," the woman says to hot-dog guy.

Come on, people, back to me. Focus.

"Yes, I have quit the talent quest," I say, louder. "Would you like to know why?"

The woman nods slowly. "Uh-huh, sure."

"I am quitting the talent quest to focus on finding my missing grandpa."

As soon as I say the word "grandpa," every head on the lawn snaps in my direction. Suddenly the leftover hamburger appears to have gotten more interesting to these pigeons.

The woman in front of me pulls a photo out of a folder she's holding. "This is a photo of Walter Walburt ..." she says, and then raises her eyebrows as though she wants me to finish the sentence.

"Yes, that's my grandpa. Walter Walburt. Shocking choice of name, right? I mean, what were his parents thinking?"

She looks at me quizzically, as though she doesn't care at all about that.

"Yes, well, he's gone missing. At least I'm pretty sure Mom and Dad didn't find him last night," I continue. "Wait. Why do you have a photo of Grandpa?"

She looks across at the other reporters, not sure whether she should tell me.

Beard guy shrugs. "He asked you." She doesn't seem convinced though.

"You should probably go get your mom or dad," she says to me.

"I'm his dad," comes a deep voice from behind me, and I nearly jump out of my skin. "You shouldn't be talking to my son. What do you want?"

Dad's got his serious voice on. Told you he doesn't like to be woken up.

To these pigeons, Dad is one huge, juicy, untouched hamburger combo deal. They actually run at him, microphones outstretched.

"What are you talking about?" Dad asks. "What ransom?"

"Someone dropped a ransom note into the Channel Eleven office this morning," beard guy says, pulling a piece of paper out of his folder. Dad snatches it.

"Are you telling us you don't know about this?"

What's going on? Grandpa has been kidnapped? A ransom?

Dad reads the note quickly and then turns a little pale. He looks back at the reporters. "We don't have any comments at this stage."

He pulls Hugo and me back inside, leaving the reporters with only Duck to talk to. I'm sure he'll keep them occupied.

Mom is standing in the kitchen wrapped in her dressing gown and holding Rosie.

Without saying a word, Dad puts the piece of paper on the table.

Dear ciTizens of rEdhill!
I have kiDnapped WAlter F. WalBurt.
He is not hURt.
I am FinDing him to be
vERY SMART.
And we're hAving some Lovely
cONverSation.

I do want ONE MIlliOn
dollars though. You might
need to run a fund-raiser,
so BettEr hop to it.
Bring the money to
Redhill ParK at 8 p.m.
YouRS SinCereLy,
The KidnaPper

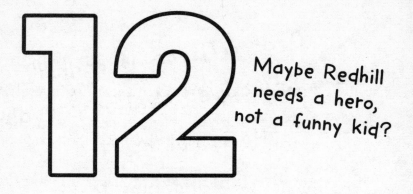

12

Maybe Redhill needs a hero, not a funny kid?

I can't believe Mom and Dad send Hugo and me to school. I think they do it just to get us out of their hair. They seem to think that two eleven-year-olds aren't going to be helpful or something.

Hmpf. I'll show them.

Forget the stupid talent quest. Now we have something much more important to focus on. My grandpa has been kidnapped and I'm probably going to be on the news!

I don't know anyone else whose grandpa has been kidnapped. Apparently it's quite rare. So Mom and Dad can discount me all they like, but if there's ever been an opportunity to become the hero of Redhill, this is it, and I'm going to make the most of it by rescuing Grandpa myself.

At lunchtime I gather my task force in the library.

TASK FORCE
CODE NAME:
GRANDPA
TOP SECRET MEETING: LIBRARY

"What is a task force?" Hugo asks as he ushers Kevin, Layla, and Ryan into the study room.

"It's like the Avengers," I explain. "Or the Justice League."

"So you're Batman and I'm Superman?" He's a sweet kid.

"Hugo, I think if I'm Batman, then you're Alfred," I reply while laying out pieces of paper on the library table. "Couldn't do it without you though!"

Everyone sits down around the table. Nothing ever happens in Redhill, so we're all pretty excited about rescuing a grandpa.

"Can I come in?" I look up. Abby Purcell is standing in the doorway. Nothing's ever easy, is it? I'm figuring out how best to explain that rescue operations are not math tests and that maybe Abby would be better suited to the chess club meeting on the other side of the library when Hugo beats me to it.

Ugh. Hugo!

"What are all these names on the table?" Abby asks, pointing at the sheets of paper I've laid out. Each one has a different name printed on it.

"These are the suspects in Grandpa's kidnapping," I say.

She does her stupid one-eyebrow thing and holds up a piece of paper. On it I've written: *MISS SWEET*.

YOU THINK OUR TEACHER TOOK YOUR GRANDPA?

"It's important not to rule out anyone this early in an investigation."

"So everyone's guilty until proven innocent?" Abby asks.

"That's what they say," I reply.

"It couldn't possibly be Miss Sweet," Ryan says. "She's the nicest person I've ever met in my entire life."

"She put a star sticker on my homework this morning," Layla says. "She was in such a good mood."

"We had homework?" I ask.

"What about this guy?" Kevin picks up another piece of paper. "Who's Rupert?"

Abby laughs. "You think the stage manager from the talent quest took your grandpa?"

"You never know!"

She lifts up a different paper. "Who's Dr. Duncanbray?"

"He works at the nursing home. There's something very suspicious about that doctor," I say. He's currently my prime suspect, just because he was so close to where the crime occurred.

"And he has a lot of teeth," Hugo adds. "Like more teeth than a normal person."

"Who's Breakfast-Hot-Dog Guy?" Ryan asks.

"One of the journalists," I say.

"I think it was him," Hugo says. "I mean, who needs a hot dog for breakfast?"

"Duck certainly didn't trust him and he has an instinct for that sort of thing. He could have kidnapped Grandpa just so he had a good story to write about in his newspaper," I say.

Layla nods. "That makes sense."

"He does have a motive," says Kevin.

"Good to know we're all in agreement, then." I pick up all the pieces of paper as the bell rings for the end of lunch. "Hugo and I will take this information to the police station after school."

Abby shakes her head.

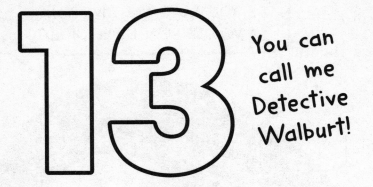

13

You can call me Detective Walburt!

I've never been inside Redhill Police Station before. Abby made some comment at school about how I should get to know it because I'll probably spend a lot of time there one day. She's so dumb. I don't want to be a policeman.

Hugo and I walk up to the front desk. There is a cop with very big muscles sitting behind a computer. He's sucking on some sort of purple drink through a straw, and I think the drink is going straight into his arms and inflating them. He smiles when he sees us.

"What can I do for you two champs?"

He must realize that we're going to help him

solve the case and he'll probably get the rest of the afternoon off.

"We're here to see Sergeant Purcell," I say.

Standard response. Perhaps he doesn't realize how important we are. That's okay, I can tell him.

"In this case, I think she'll want you to interrupt her," I suggest.

"In this case, I think, um … no." He grins and sucks on his straw.

"But we have important suspects she needs to investigate," Hugo tries.

"You should leave those suspects with me, then," he says, pointing to a tray full of papers on his desk and going back to looking at his computer.

LISTEN, MR. POLICEMAN. I KNOW SERGEANT PURCELL'S DAUGHTER, AND IF HER MOM IS ANYTHING LIKE HER, THEN SHE'S GOING TO TURN INTO A REAL WEREWOLF IF YOU MAKE HER CRANKY. ARE YOU SURE YOU WANT TO RISK THAT?

He's still grinning.

"Seriously," I say. "I'm sure you're very brave, Mr. Policeman, but there's bravery and then there's insanity. No one gets medals for insanity."

He seems to be finding us quite amusing. Not really the response I'm going for.

"I'll take my chances, thanks, boys."

Okay. I've had about enough of this.

"But we have suspects! Suspects for the Walter Walburt kidnapping! What sort of operation are you running here?"

"Walter Walburt? He's that old guy, right?"

"Excuse me!" Hugo exclaims. "That 'old guy' is his grandpa!"

Mr. Policeman looks at me. "You're Walter Walburt's grandson?"

Finally! We're getting somewhere. "As I was saying, we think we have a few leads ..."

"Do you know where your parents are right now, kid?" He's still not listening to me. I can't believe this guy gets paid with my tax dollars.

"Don't tell us they've been kidnapped too!" Hugo gasps.

Mr. Policeman laughs and stands up. "No, no. But they are here."

Hugo grabs my shoulders. "Max! They've arrested your parents!"

The police officer leaves his purple drink on the desk and, chuckling to himself, begins to walk down the corridor. "Come with me, boys."

We follow him down a hallway, through a room with lots of desks, past a few jail cells with some funny-looking dudes inside, and up to a door that has Sergeant Purcell's name on it. Mr. Policeman knocks and then opens the door.

"Mr. and Mrs. Walburt, your son is here," he says.

So Sergeant Purcell is in a meeting. With my mom and dad.

"What are you boys doing here? You were supposed to go straight home after school," Mom says.

"We have some suspects in Grandpa's kidnapping," I say, and slap my handful of papers down onto Sergeant Purcell's desk.

THANKS, MAX.
WHO'S YOUR LEADING SUSPECT?

Out of the corner of my eye, I can see my parents silently apologizing for my initiative. Thanks, guys. I thought we were a team.

"His name is Breakfast-Hot-Dog Guy," I say.

THAT'S NOT HIS REAL NAME.

"Okay, thanks, boys," Dad says, rising from his chair and putting one hand on each of our shoulders. "Time for you to head home."

"I think you have your talent quest meeting tonight, right?" Mom asks. "You don't want to be late for that."

"I quit, remember? Anyway, we need to keep working on rescuing Grandpa from the kidnappers."

Sergeant Purcell steps in. "Max, we actually don't think your grandpa has been kidnapped."

"What do you mean? I saw the ransom note."

"We think someone was playing a not-very-funny joke. There were a lot of things that didn't make sense about the note."

"So we're not going to pay the million dollars?" I ask.

Sergeant Purcell shakes her head. "Some of my officers will still go to the park tonight, just in case. But we can't see any reason why someone would have kidnapped your grandpa."

Dad uses his grip on our shoulders to steer us out of the office and all the way back out of the police station.

"But, Dad, what about Breakfast-Hot-Dog Guy?" I ask.

Dad gives a huge sigh. "We'll look into it, Max. We'll look into it."

No, they won't.

14

I'm operating on a whole other level!

Dad tells us we need to go to our talent quest meeting at the town hall or go home. I say we'll go to the meeting, but only because I'm hatching a totally different plan that he doesn't need to know about.

"I don't understand," Hugo says as he, Duck, and I walk down the main street of Redhill.

"What don't you understand, Hugo?" I ask. "The meaning of life? Whether a whale ever gets a runny blowhole?"

"Why we're going to a meeting for all the people in the talent quest if … you've quit the talent quest?"

"Well, I haven't officially quit."

"So you're still going to compete in it?"

NO CHANCE. MY DAYS AS THE FUNNY KID ARE OVER. I DON'T HAVE TIME TO BE A COMEDIAN WHEN THERE'S ALL THIS IMPORTANT DETECTIVE WORK TO DO.

THEN WHY ARE WE GOING TO THE MEETING?

Poor Hugo. He's a little on edge.

"We're going to the meeting so that we can sneak out and catch the kidnapper," I explain.

"What?"

"Haven't you been paying attention? Remember the ransom note? The kidnapper is going to be at Redhill Park at eight p.m. to collect the million dollars. We're going to be there too."

We walk up the steps to the front door of the town hall. All the other contestants are arriving too – the horse guy, the opera singer, Abby the stupid magician. I even see Tumbles walking across the parking lot from the warehouse next door. Oh, boy, I would love to beat all these people – do I really need to quit?

I shake my head. Yes, yes, you do. Stay focused, Max. Hugo, it turns out, is talking.

"But the police don't think the ransom note is real. Sergeant Purcell –"

I interrupt. "Sergeant Purcell said the police were going to be there anyway, which tells you something, doesn't it?"

"Does it?"

"Regardless, between Sergeant Purcell and Mr. Purple Juice at the front desk, I'm no longer convinced the police are up to the task of rescuing Grandpa. It's up to us now, Hugo."

"I don't think your dad would like this plan."

"Oh, he'd hate it."

* * * *

The talent quest meeting is a complete waste of time. Rupert tells us how Saturday night's event is going to run – what time to be there, where to stand, that the stage lights mean we need to wear makeup (no way). I don't have to know any of this, because I'm going to tell Rupert I quit.

Rupert is standing on the stage, which we all know is where he wants to be. The contestants are sitting in the front row of the hall while he parades around in front of us under the lights.

YOU HAVE TO UNDERSTAND, THE WHOLE TOWN WILL BE HERE! TWO HUNDRED PEOPLE! THREE HUNDRED PEOPLE! TEN THOUSAND PEOPLE! YOU WILL ENTERTAIN THEM AND THEY WILL LOVE YOU FOR IT!

"I don't think you'll get ten thousand people in here, Rupert, poppet," Tumbles calls out from the back row. For some reason, the stupid clown is too cool to sit with the rest of us. Fine with me!

Rupert snaps out of his rant and brushes his chest with his hands as though he's dropped crumbs on his shirt and he's trying to get them off.

NO, NO, OF COURSE, YOU'RE PROBABLY RIGHT. IT WILL BE MORE LIKE TWO HUNDRED. I GOT A LITTLE CARRIED AWAY.

Ugh. How much longer till we can leave?

"My point is," Rupert continues, "you've likely never been in front of an audience this big before. You won't have heard cheering this loud or had so many pairs of eyes watching your every move, listening to your every word …"

I glance up and around the seats. I hate to admit it, but Rupert is onto something. It would feel pretty amazing to be up on that stage. The whole town of Redhill will be here.

Maybe I don't really need to quit …

> HI THERE, UNFUNNY KID!

Forget it! I instantly remember all the reasons why I decided to quit. I turn to Hugo. I need to stay focused. The funny kid is gone. I've got more important things to do, like catch a kidnapper!

> LET'S GET OUT OF HERE.

"Where are you guys going?" Abby asks. "The meeting hasn't finished yet!"

But Hugo and I are already on our way out.

15 Live life on the hedge!

It's dark outside as Hugo and I run down the front steps of the town hall and, joined by Duck, head toward Redhill Park.

"Where are you idiots going?"

Oh, no, she's following us! Abby Purcell, my personal bad dream, is running down the steps behind us. Just ignore her and keep going! That's my motto.

Hugo, on the other hand, stops and starts to explain. "We're going to –"

"Don't engage with her, Hugo!" I say. "Just keep running."

"Keep running where?" Abby asks.

"The –"

Why does Hugo always feel like he needs to answer her when she asks him a question?

SHE'S LIKE A FART, HUGO! IF YOU IGNORE HER FOR LONG ENOUGH, SHE'LL GO AWAY!

"Oh, really, Max? I'm like a ... fart?" She speeds up to reach my side and then settles into a jog. I'm focused on the footpath and getting to Redhill Park, but out of the corner of my eye, I can see her glaring at me. It's very off-putting.

Aaaaarrrrrrrggggggggggghhhhhhhhhhhh!

"All right! I'll tell you!" I yell. "We're going to buy ice cream."

"You are the worst liar ever."

She's so annoying that I almost don't realize we've arrived at Redhill Park.

"Get down!" I say, and grab Hugo and Duck, pulling them into a hedge.

Abby stops in the middle of the footpath and looks very confused. "Why did you just climb into a hedge?"

She is going to ruin everything! If the kidnapper sees us, they won't make an appearance at the park. Then we'll never be able to rescue Grandpa.

"Abby, either get in here with us, or go away! Right now, I don't care which!"

She cocks her head slightly to the side. "You want me to climb into that hedge with you guys?"

I can hear footsteps. Someone is coming down the path!

"It's either this hedge or that garbage bin over there. Quick!"

I can tell Abby hears the footsteps too. She's thinking it over ... thinking it over ... thinking it –

"Oh, come on!" I groan.

She jumps into the hedge. "Why do I always seem to end up in some sort of shrubbery with you guys?" she grumbles.

The footsteps are very close now.

"Trust me," I whisper. "I hate it as much as you do."

"Really?" Hugo says. "I quite like it. It's so snuggly."

SHHHHH! HERE THEY COME!

I would like to interrupt this moment to say that putting your hand over someone's mouth when they are trying to talk is rude and an invasion of personal space and, well, basically you should never ever do it.

Unless ... it's an extremely, EXTREMELY specific circumstance. That one specific circumstance when it is okay to put your hand over someone's mouth to silence them is when:

1. Your grandpa has been kidnapped.
2. You are hiding in a hedge to try to catch the kidnapper.
3. Abby Purcell is hiding in that hedge with you, but doesn't really know why.
4. Abby Purcell decides to speak very loudly because she just saw her mom.

The other thing that's important to note is that if you find yourself in this exact situation and you do what I just did – cover someone's mouth with your hand – then you have no idea what could happen next.

Abby glares at me with eyes that look like fiery asteroids that are just about to explode into my face. She puts both hands on my shoulders and, with the strength of the Incredible Hulk and Optimus Prime's baby, shoves me straight out of the hedge. I go flying through the air, flip twice, and end up sprawled on the footpath.

Yep. I probably deserved that.

Only now we have a much bigger problem.

Sergeant Purcell hears the splat of my face on the concrete and turns around as Abby and Hugo step out of the hedge and Duck does a runner. Her eyes go very wide, very quickly.

WHAT ARE YOU KIDS DOING HERE?

Which is how Abby, Hugo, and I find ourselves locked in the back of a police car while the cops check the park for any sign of the kidnapper.

None of us is talking to each other, unless you count Hugo's tummy rumbling. I don't know what's going on in there, but his intestines seem to have sensed a gap in the conversation and now have a lot to say.

Abby's mad because I got her in trouble with her mom. I'm mad because Abby ruined my face and my chance of catching the kidnapper and rescuing Grandpa. Hugo is mad because … I don't know why Hugo is mad. I think he's just hungry. That must be what his tummy is yabbering on about. We did miss dinner.

After a long time, Sergeant Purcell gets back in the car and starts the engine.

"Did you catch the kidnapper? Did you rescue Grandpa?" I ask.

Something's happened to Sergeant Purcell's eyebrows. They seem to be stuck in a V shape. There's some crazy eyebrow DNA in this family.

"No, Max. As I told you at the police station, we think the ransom note was fake. We were just here to make sure. It's very important that you leave this job to us. This is not a job for kids, okay? I'm taking you home to your parents."

Under different circumstances, it probably would have been quite exciting to get a ride in a police car. Instead I have to sit next to Abby Purcell and endure conversations like:

"Max, if I can offer you some advice …"

"I'd really rather you didn't."

"It's just that now that you're quitting things you're terrible at, I think you should probably add 'detective' to your list."

There's this thing they call solitary confinement that sounds amazing right now.

17

Don't you dream in comic book form?

Mom and Dad are super mad. But they also say nice things like, "We know you're worried about Grandpa" and "We understand you were just trying to help" and "You boys often do very stupid things when you're hungry."

But mostly they say, "We will find Grandpa. You need to leave it to the grown-ups. You mustn't try to find Grandpa by yourself again."

Then they send us to bed. I fall asleep thinking about the fact that I forgot to quit the talent quest while we were at the meeting and that it looked very cool up on that stage tonight.

Then I have a nightmare about Tumbles.

18

A plan of pure genius!

(If I do say so myself!)

Hugo and I get ready for school early.

I run around the house like a crazy person trying to find everything I need to solve all of my life's problems, and Hugo walks around slowly, saying things like, "What are you doing?" and "I don't understand" and "Have you seen my pants?"

Once we find his pants, I drag him out of the house, but instead of walking toward the bus stop, we start the long walk toward Redhill Nursing Home.

"Why are we going this way?" Hugo asks.

Duck waddles along beside us.

"Last night I had a dream," I begin.

"Me too! I dreamt I was sleeping inside a lasagna," Hugo says. "I was so warm."

Weird.

"Last night Abby kept calling me a quitter. I didn't like that. I'm not a quitter. You don't think I'm a quitter, do you?"

"Well, you did quit the talent quest ..."

"Exactly. That's why I've changed my mind."

"You're not quitting the talent quest now?"
Hugo asks.

"I am not quitting the talent quest."

"So that's what your dream was about? Not quitting?"

"No, no. My dream was about winning the talent quest!"

"Were you funnier than Tumbles in your dream?" Hugo asks.

"My dream was about Grandpa too."

"What does your grandpa have to do with the talent quest?"

"Everything, Hugo. Everything."

"I'm so confused," Hugo says. "Your mom, your dad, the police, pretty much everyone has said that we're not allowed to try and find your grandpa anymore. As your life coach, I need to tell you to leave it to the professionals."

"You are not my life coach, Hugo, and we are

not going to find Grandpa. If Mom and Dad and Sergeant Purcell want to do that by themselves, then that's fine. Grandpa was never very nice to me anyway, and I have bigger challenges."

Hugo blinks. "Max, I'm not understanding anything you're saying."

THAT'S OKAY, HUGO. I DON'T EXPECT YOU TO ALWAYS BE ABLE TO KEEP UP. GRANDPA CAN STILL HELP ME WIN THE TALENT QUEST, EVEN IF WE DON'T FIND HIM.

Hugo rubs his head with his hands. "I just want to go back and crawl inside my lasagna. Life was so much simpler then. How can your missing grandpa help you win the talent quest?"

I leave a pause for dramatic effect.

"Because, Hugo, my friend, we're going to convince everyone that Tumbles the clown kidnapped him."

It's the work of a genius. Duck quacks. He clearly agrees.

"You think Tumbles kidnapped your grandpa?"

"Oh, no. Of course not," I reply. "But if we make people think he did, and the police are investigating him, then we might be able to get him kicked out of the talent quest. And if Tumbles is out, then I'll be the only funny one. And funny always wins."

"But how would we ever convince people that Tumbles kidnapped your grandpa?"

I open up my backpack and Hugo looks inside.

"Hey, that's my flower," he says.

"It's one of Tumbles's plastic flowers. And we're going to hide it at Redhill Nursing Home."

Hugo stops. His eyes go wide and he starts shaking his head.

"The police will find it, and I don't know about you, Hugo, but I've only seen one clown in Redhill."

Hugo is looking very worried.

NO, MAX.

YES, HUGO.

NO ... MAX.

YES ... HUGO.

MAX, YOU CAN'T DO THAT!

He tries to grab my backpack. I yank it back. "Of course *we* can. And it'll work too. We could even give Breakfast-Hot-Dog Guy a call with an anonymous tip and he'll do all the work for us. Tumbles the clown will be history!"

"But ... that's not right, Max. Your grandpa is missing. He might be in danger, and all you can think about is that you might be able to use that to help you win the talent quest? I know Tumbles ruined your act, but this is too much."

I'LL TELL YOU WHAT'S TOO MUCH, HUGO. EVER SINCE THAT TALENT QUEST AUDITION, EVERYTHING HAS GONE WRONG. AND NONE OF IT IS MY FAULT. TUMBLES RUINED MY ACT! PEOPLE KEEP CALLING ME THE UNFUNNY KID! I GOT TAKEN HOME IN A POLICE CAR! WELL, ENOUGH'S ENOUGH. IT'S TIME FOR ME TO FIX THINGS. TUMBLES NEEDS TO GO SO I CAN BE THE FUNNY KID AGAIN.

"What about your grandpa? Everyone's worried about him, but you're thinking about how his disappearance might be able to help you ... cheat."

"Well …" I stumble for the best words. "Um … I don't know if I'd call it … cheating."

Hugo's eyes narrow. I don't know if he's ever glared at me like this before. If he wants me to keep being his best friend, he's got a funny way of showing it.

"It's definitely cheating, Max." Then Hugo folds his arms. "I know your grandpa isn't very nice, Max, but neither are you. If you do this, I'm going to … quit being your life coach."

Well, that makes things easy, doesn't it.

"You're not my life coach, Hugo!"

He stares at me. "Apparently. Not."

And then he turns around and walks back down the street.

"Hugo?" I call after him. "Hugo!"

But he ignores me.

I look down at my feathered friend.

19

You're on, Captain KickDUCK!

Duck and I head around the back of the nursing home.

I thought the backyard would be empty first thing in the morning. Turns out old people must have breakfast at five a.m., because by seven thirty a.m. they're all sitting outside, having their first nap of the day.

Up at the top of the garden I can see Dr. Duncanbray, or rather I can see the morning sun reflecting off all his teeth.

Duck and I squat in the bushes. I spend a lot of time in bushes. I put the plastic flower in his beak and then point up the hill to Dr. Duncanbray.

OKAY, DUCK. YOU'RE THE KEY TO THIS. I KNOW YOU WON'T LET ME DOWN. SEE THAT CREEPY GUY WITH THE GIANT WHITE MOUTH? GIVE THIS FLOWER TO HIM.

Duck looks at me blankly. Oh, I wish I could speak quack.

"Um … flower … give … creepy doctor."

Still nothing.

I don't think it's that he doesn't understand me. He's just looking at me like he needs something.

"What do you want, Duck?"

He cocks his head to the side as though he's saying, "I shouldn't have to tell you." Oh, I hate these games. Um …

"Duck, you know I love you, right … ?"

That was it! Duck's off!

I watch as he run-waddles across the grass. Poor little guy. Must have gotten a bit frightened after my fight with Hugo. I've never seen Hugo like that. He normally just does whatever I tell him. I guess he feels strongly about this.

HEY, THERE'S A DUCK AT TWELVE O'CLOCK!

I look up and see Sir Phillip Bartholomew the Third standing on his deck chair and pointing his walking stick at Duck. I wonder how Grandpa is going without his new walking stick.

Duck's way too fast for Sir Phillip. He runs around the chairs, under a table, and then between the legs of the old lady I met the other day. She looks through her legs and calls after him, "Are you Cyril?"

Duck runs all the way up to Dr. Duncanbray and drops the yellow flower at his feet.

Is Hugo right? Is this a really bad thing to be doing? Have I gone too far?

Dr. Duncanbray picks up the yellow flower and then seems to give it a little squeeze. The flower squirts water straight in his face!

That thing was filled with water! I had no idea. So that's why Tumbles gave it to me after my act. It was a booby trap!

Oh, that stupid clown! That's it. I almost thought better of this plan, but I should have known better.

That clown is going down.

20

Hugo seems to be losing his hearing, poor fella.

To be honest, I have no idea if this plan will actually work. Dr. Duncanbray might go back inside and chuck the yellow flower in the trash ... or he might give Sergeant Purcell a call.

I guess I just have to wait and see.

When I get to school, I call out to Hugo, but he doesn't hear me. In class, I ask him to give me the answers to the homework, but he doesn't hear me then either. Weird. After lunch, when Miss Sweet is reading to us, I throw an eraser at Hugo to get his attention, but he just asks Miss Sweet if he can go to the bathroom. I'm beginning to think he might be ignoring me.

He doesn't even say anything when we walk from the bus stop. This is getting ridiculous.

"Hugo! Are you ever going to talk to me again?"

He stops on the front step and looks at me. "Are you still trying to make it look like Tumbles kidnapped your grandpa?"

"Of course I —"

Hugo walks inside.

Man! What's a kid got to do around here to get some loyalty from his friends?

TONIGHT YOU'RE SLEEPING ON THE COUCH.

* * * *

When I wake up the next morning, I can hear Sergeant Purcell talking to my parents downstairs. I stumble out.

Mom and Dad are sitting across from Sergeant Purcell in the lounge room. The further we get into this week, the more tired my parents are beginning to look. Their faces have gone a weird shade of gray and they've started missing things. Like the fact that Rosie is playing with the ...

"Power outlet!" I yell, and quickly grab Rosie's hand, pulling it away from the power socket.

Mom and Dad turn their heads slowly, like sloths.

"Oh. Thanks, Max," Dad says.

That's when I see what's sitting on the coffee table in front of them. It's the yellow plastic flower.

"What is that?" I ask carefully.

Sergeant Purcell answers. "It was found at your grandpa's nursing home, Max. It looks like some sort of party toy, but when you squeeze it, it squirts water, which makes me think it's from a clown or children's entertainer or something. No one at the nursing home had ever seen it before, so I thought I'd ask your parents if they recognize it. Just in case it has anything to do with your grandpa's disappearance." She turns back to my parents. "I knew it was a long shot, but I thought I'd ask anyway."

My parents nod. I guess this is my moment.

"I've seen that before," I say.

All three of them turn and look at me.

"Where?" Sergeant Purcell asks.

"The clown who is in the talent quest with me. He has a whole bunch of them."

"There's a clown in the talent quest?" Mom asks.

"Yeah. He's pretty mean too. His name is Tumbles."

My parents look back at Sergeant Purcell.

She shrugs. "It would be good to talk to him, then. Do you know where he lives, Max?"

I shake my head. "No, but he'll be at the rehearsal tonight. I could introduce you so you can have a chat with him, if you like?"

The police officer nods slowly.

My dad is rubbing his temples, clearly thinking about something.

"Do you think Tumbles had something to do with Grandpa going missing?" I ask.

"Oh, probably not, Max," says Sergeant Purcell. "But in police work, it's important to follow every lead. I might pop along to the rehearsal tonight and have a little chat with Tumbles."

I nod and turn to go to the bathroom. Hugo

is standing at the end of the hallway, watching
me. Then he bows his head and walks into the
bathroom, jumping the line.

As I stand there trying to hold it, I hear Dad
mumbling to himself.

TUMBLES. TUMBLES. WHERE
HAVE I HEARD THAT BEFORE?

Those guys are
seriously tired.

21

Yoo-hoo! Where are you, little clownie-wownie?

Mom and Dad can't take me to the rehearsal tonight, because they have a meeting with, of all people, Breakfast-Hot-Dog Guy! There's going to be a big article in Saturday's newspaper about Grandpa's disappearance. Apparently it might even make the front page. Who would ever think Grandpa would be famous?

Hugo doesn't want to come with me either, because he says he has a sore tummy. Yeah, right! That's fine. I don't need him anyway.

When I arrive at the town hall, Sergeant Purcell and Abby are waiting for me on the front steps.

GOT ALL YOUR JOKES READY, MAX?

"Of course I do," I reply. Actually, I've only got a couple of ideas, but I figure as long as I can get rid of Tumbles, this rehearsal should be a piece of cake. I look up at Sergeant Purcell. "Let me show you which one is Tumbles."

"Does he have a giant red nose?"

"Sure does."

"And a funny little hat?"

"Yep."

"And enormous shoes?" she asks.

"They are pretty big."

"Is there more than one clown in the talent quest?"

"Nope. Just Tumbles."

"Then that's probably him over there, then," Sergeant Purcell says with a wink.

I turn to look over my shoulder and, sure enough, Tumbles is walking up toward the front door. "Ah, yes."

Abby smirks. "My mom is a very good detective."

"Excuse me, sir!" Sergeant Purcell calls out to Tumbles. "Do you mind if we have a quick chat?"

Tumbles stops and stares across at us. I imagine we must look a bit odd – a pretend

magician, a police officer, and a genius comedian all standing together.

He slowly points to his chest as if to say, "Who, me?"

"Yes, you. You're Tumbles the clown, correct?" Sergeant Purcell calls across the steps.

Tumbles stands very still and his mouth opens a little, but not to tell a joke. He reminds me of Rosie when she's in trouble with Mom.

"I just want to ask you a few questions about Walter Walburt," Sergeant Purcell says.

Tumbles' eyes open wide. It looks as if he might know Grandpa's name.

Then he turns.

And runs!

"Hey! Stop right there!" Sergeant Purcell yells, but Tumbles keeps running.

Abby and I actually look at each other in shock. Even I know you should never run away from a police officer if they want to talk to you. Whatever is going on, Tumbles does not want to talk to the police.

He runs inside the town hall. Sergeant Purcell follows and Abby runs after her.

Suddenly I can't figure out what's going on. I didn't actually think Tumbles had anything to do with Grandpa going missing. Duck and I put the flower at Redhill Nursing Home. That was the whole reason Hugo was mad at me! I'm making it look like Tumbles had something to do with Grandpa's disappearance, even though he didn't.

But Tumbles certainly looked like he knew Grandpa's name when Sergeant Purcell said it. Then he ran away! And he wouldn't run away unless he was … guilty?

Have I just found Grandpa's kidnapper … by accident?

22 The stage is mine!

Half an hour later, I'm standing on the stage for my turn in the rehearsal.

"I thought I saw Tumbles earlier," Rupert says. "But he's disappeared."

"He's in trouble with the police," I mumble. I'm still in shock over what happened. Has Tumbles really kidnapped my grandpa?

WHAT'S THAT?

HE'S IN TROUBLE WITH THE POLICE. ABBY'S MOM IS LOOKING FOR HIM.

Rupert looks a little stunned and then glances down at his clipboard. "Well, okay then. I guess that rules him out." I watch him cross Tumbles's name off his list. Then he looks up at me. "It seems like you're it, funny kid."

This is exactly what I wanted. Tumbles is out. I can win this thing now ... but it doesn't feel like I thought it would. I keep thinking about Grandpa.

"Take it away, Max."

I look down at the piece of paper I'm holding, where I've scrawled a few jokes.

Come on, be a professional, I tell myself. Get this done and then work out what to do about Tumbles later. You can do this. You are the funny kid. You're great at making people laugh. Do your stuff! Now there's no reason not to get that mojo back!

I clear my throat.

AH, GOOD EVENING, EVERYONE. I'M SURE YOU'VE ALL HEARD THE JOKE ABOUT WHY THE CHICKEN CROSSED THE ROAD, BUT HAVE YOU HEARD THE ONE ABOUT WHY THE CHICKEN CROSSED THE HIGHWAY? NO? NOPE? BECAUSE HE WANTED TO BE A CHICKEN NUGGET.

I know there are not many people in the hall, but there is complete silence. This suddenly feels very familiar. I keep going.

> WHY DID THE BEE, THE SOY BEAN, AND THE CHICKEN CROSS THE HIGHWAY? BECAUSE THEY WANTED TO MAKE HONEY-SOY CHICKEN.

I look at Rupert. I think he's about to cry. I better explain the joke to him.

> IT'S BECAUSE THEY'RE GETTING RUN OVER. THEY'RE GETTING SQUASHED. WHICH IS WHAT WOULD CERTAINLY HAPPEN IF A CHICKEN CROSSED A HIGHWAY ...

Okay, Rupert actually is crying now. He sits down in the front row and buries his head in his hands.

"My talent quest is going to be a disaster!" he sobs.

"It's okay, I've got m-more," I stammer. "Um, why did the chicken play drums in the middle of the highway? Because he wanted to become a –"

STOP! PLEASE JUST STOP!

"Drumstick," I finish weakly.

Rupert throws all his papers and his clipboard up into the air and marches toward the door.

TOMORROW NIGHT THIS HALL WILL BE FILLED WITH THE WHOLE TOWN AND MY SHOW IS FALLING APART! WHY CAN'T THERE BE SOME ACTUAL TALENT IN THIS TALENT QUEST? TOMORROW THERE WON'T BE SILENCE, THERE'LL BE BOOS!

He storms out.

I stand all alone in the middle of the stage until I hear footsteps approaching. It's Abby Purcell, surely coming to rub my failure in my face. She'll be right too. Even without Tumbles, I'm not funny anymore. The funny kid, just like my grandpa, has disappeared.

So come on, Abby Purcell. Hit me with it.

Instead she just puts one hand on my shoulder and says, "It'll be okay, Max. It'll be okay."

It's the middle of the night and Hugo is back sleeping on a trundle bed in my bedroom, because Rosie wet herself on the couch.

Hugo doesn't reply, but that doesn't tell me much, because Hugo has been ignoring me for two days now. He might still be ignoring me. Or he could be asleep.

"Well, if you can hear me, Hugo, you were right. I've been way more worried about finding 'funny kid' than I have about finding Grandpa."

There's still silence. Hugo's probably dreaming about being inside a lasagna again.

"I think Tumbles really might have Grandpa. And now all I can think about is that Grandpa is stuck somewhere with that stupid clown and no one knows where he is."

I think I hear Hugo shuffle in his trundle bed.

"The talent quest can wait. I need to rescue Grandpa first, but to do that … I'm gonna need my life coach back."

Slowly Hugo peeks up at me over the side of my mattress with a smile on his face.

* * * *

Hugo and I leave straight after breakfast and head to the town hall. We decide that if we're going to try to work out where Tumbles might have gone, it's best we start at the last place we saw him.

"You know who would be really helpful?" Hugo says.

"Who?"

"Steve. We should call Steve."

"We are NOT calling Steve! That dog hates me!" I shout.

"But he would be really good at finding Tu–"

"I thought we weren't going to find Tumbles, Hugo. You were very bossy about how we are just going to try to work out where he could have gone and then tell Mom and Dad."

"Yes, yes. You're right," Hugo replies. "We're just trying to solve the mystery. We're not going to do anything dangerous."

"I would be happy to go have a little look, if we think we know where he's hiding –"

"No, Max! We agreed –"

"Okay, okay. We're here."

I take Hugo to the place I last saw Tumbles, which is the front door of the town hall. We try the door, but it's locked.

"The mysterious thing," I say to Hugo, "is that if Tumbles is a clown who doesn't want to be found, then he can't really be seen moving around Redhill. He can't catch a bus. He can't walk to the town hall for the talent quest."

"So he must be somewhere pretty close to here. Do you think he's living in the town hall?" Hugo asks as we walk around the side of the building. "He could have a little hideout backstage somewhere."

"He could. That's what I would do," I reply.

"No, actually, that wouldn't make sense," Hugo says. "Because we saw him walking across the parking lot from that old warehouse that time."

I stop. Hugo's right! I forgot about that.

Across the parking lot beside the town hall

is an old, empty warehouse. I look at Hugo. "Do you think …"

"… Tumbles is living in the warehouse?" Hugo finishes my sentence.

Before Hugo can work out what he thinks about that idea, I run across the parking lot toward the old building. Sure enough, there's a door on the side with a little brick stopping it from closing completely.

About three hours later, Hugo catches up, totally out of breath.

"Okay, Max … time to go get your mom and dad … so that they can call … the police," Hugo puffs.

"But we don't even know if he's in there," I say. "Sergeant Purcell already thinks we're just stupid kids. We can't call her if he's not even in there. Let's just have a quick look."

"Max, no –"

I push the door open a little and lean inside. It's really dark in there, like we're wearing sunglasses and a blindfold while walking into a cave that's been painted black.

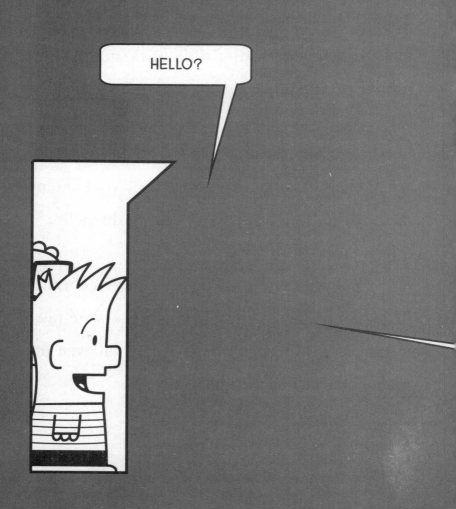

"*Maaaaxxxxxx*," Hugo whispers through clenched teeth.

There's a noise from the other side of the room, like someone bumping into something.

WHO'S THERE?

We both freeze. We can't see who said it, but recognize the voice. Tumbles!

Hugo whispers to me:

LET'S GET OUT OF HERE!

"We can't!" I whisper back.

"Why not?"

"Because he knows we've found him."

"So?"

"He'll run away!"

It's quite tricky to have a whisper argument.

"So what are we supposed to do?"

"We have to answer him!" I whisper back. "We have to pretend to be other people so we don't spook him!"

"Who are we going to pretend to be?"

"Um –" Quick. I need to think of something.

I'M ... CAPTAIN KICKBUTT.

Ugh. Dumb answer. Hugo slaps himself on the forehead and groans.

There's silence from inside. My eyes are starting to adjust to the darkness a little. I think I can see Tumbles sitting on a stool in the far corner.

"Max? Is that you?" Tumbles asks.

Uh-oh.

Suddenly I see Tumbles reach out his arm and flick on a lamp.

The light blinds me at first.

Hugo gasps.

I squint and realize that the man sitting on the stool isn't Tumbles at all.

It's Grandpa.

24

Wait. What?

"Grandpa?"

"Hello, Max," he says, standing. It appears that he's made a little bedroom for himself. There's a mattress on the floor, a few cardboard boxes for a table, and a big piece of broken mirror balancing against the wall. Next to the mirror is the Tumbles costume.

My eyes go wide.

Tumbles the clown is ... Grandpa?

"Wait ... what?" My brain hurts. I have been using it way too much recently.

This whole time my grumpy grandpa, who everyone has been trying to find, has been right there with me at the talent quest, covered in makeup, wearing a wig, and dressed up as a clown?

SURPRISE! YOU FOUND ME.

Hugo's jaw nearly reaches the ground.

"You boys look a little surprised. Guess I fooled you, huh?"

Hugo and I both nod as we step inside the warehouse.

"I haven't had this much fun in years." Grandpa sighs.

YOU'RE ... A CLOWN?

"You're more clever than you look, Max," Grandpa says.

"Thanks."

"I don't think that was a compliment," Hugo whispers.

"I used to dress up as Tumbles the clown all the time when I was a young man, Max," Grandpa says. "But not since your dad was a little boy. I'd forgotten how much I enjoyed it."

"Why did you stop?" I ask.

"Clowns are wonderful, but not everyone likes them. The last time I dressed up as Tumbles was for your dad's third birthday party. That was a long time ago and it was a disaster. A little boy was scared of me and ran screaming through the house. He knocked the cake over, which caused the candles to set the tablecloth on fire and burn down half our living room. I tried to put the fire out, but my cape — I used to wear a cape – caught fire too. If someone already thinks a cute clown is scary, a clown on fire is a whole other level. There was a big photo of Tumbles on the front of the local newspaper. It was pretty terrifying for everyone involved. Your grandmother made me promise that I would never dress up as Tumbles again. And I never have ..."

"Until this week?"

"Yes, well ..." Grandpa grunts and grumbles as he walks over to his Tumbles costume. "They gave me a walking stick, can you believe that? That Dr. Donkey-Butt told me I need to walk with a stick!"

I burst out laughing. "You call Dr. Duncanbray 'Dr. Donkey-Butt'?"

WOULDN'T YOU? HE HAS WAY TOO MANY TEETH.

Grandpa is funny!

"They advertised the talent quest at the nursing home and I thought maybe I could be Tumbles just one more time. I asked Dr. Donkey-Butt if I could enter and of course he said no. But I thought, you know what? What have I got to lose? Before they make me walk with a stick, take twelve pills a day, and everyone forgets about me in that nursing home, maybe we can have one last hurrah, eh? Tumbles and me? I ordered the clown suit over the phone and I just snuck out for the audition. No big deal."

"Everyone's been pretty worried about you," Hugo says.

"Oh, they'll be fine," Grandpa replies. "I never meant to be gone for the week, but it took me a while to get back to the nursing home after the audition. When I did get there, your parents had already called the police and you were out searching for me with that giant dog!"

I THOUGHT I SAW YOU IN THE BUSHES!

"Yes, well, there was no way I was coming out with that giant beast there. I hate dogs!"

"Me too!" I say.

"I knew that with everyone making such a big deal out of my disappearance, there was no way I'd be allowed to actually go in the talent quest. I'd had so much fun being Tumbles again that I didn't want to give it up. It's just a few days, I said to myself. Just a few days."

"Did you hear people thought you'd been OLDnapped?" Hugo asks.

"Yes, that was a little fun, wasn't it?" Grandpa chuckles. He holds up a copy of today's newspaper. His enormous face is on the front of it. "When I realized I was going to be 'missing' for a week, I started hiding in this old warehouse, because I didn't have to walk too far to the town hall. And then I thought, with this being Tumbles's last hurrah, maybe I should build a bit more theater around the whole thing. No one cares about an old man who's gone wandering off, but a kidnapping will get everyone's attention. So I wrote the ransom note myself and dropped it off at Channel Eleven. My plan had been to reveal my true identity in my act tonight. It might be my face on the front of the paper today, but it was going to be Tumbles's face on the front page tomorrow. What a way to finish!"

"You're a … genius," I say. "Grandpa, that's the best act ever!"

"Well, it was going to be. Until you ruined it."

Oops.

"Oh, mean-schmean. I knew Max could handle a bit of funny banter, couldn't you, Max?"

"Sure! Totally. It was fine. Didn't bother me ... at all," I reply with a gulp.

Hugo looks at me like I just grew a Pinocchio nose and my pants caught on fire.

"You're a lot like me when I was a boy, Max. I was the funny kid too. But being funny isn't easy, is it? It's hard work. When you entertain people, you're putting on a show. Always. Which means you're playing a character. You can't just stand up there and be Max telling jokes. You're a character telling jokes. People aren't just laughing at the joke, they're laughing at you. You've got to be okay with that."

"Okay ..."

Grandpa sits down. "Show me your act for tonight. I didn't get to see it yesterday."

"It's not that ... good," I admit.

"Just try," he says, and points to Hugo. "You, stand over there. You're the audience. Fire away, Max."

And so I tell him my chicken jokes, which neither he nor Hugo even smiles at, and I'm about to get to the drumstick one when Grandpa suddenly leaps up and yells:

MAX!

He scares the pants off me!

"What?"

"Oh, nothing," he says, sitting back down. "Don't worry."

But I'm completely thrown off now. "No, tell me. What?"

"It's nothing. Really. Keep going with your joke. It's gone now anyway."

"What's gone?"

Grandpa is shaking his head and his hands. "Nothing, really. I saw it above your head, but it's gone."

I look up into the warehouse above me. It's very dark up there. What is he talking about?

"What's above my head?"

"Nothing," Grandpa says again. "It dropped down behind you somewhere. Spiders are not worth worrying about."

WHAT?

THERE'S A SPIDER BEHIND ME?

Hugo chuckles a little and I glare at him. This is not a joke, you idiot.

"Well, as I said, it was above you."

"On the ceiling?"

"No, dangling from the ceiling by its web." Grandpa shrugs. "It could have dropped into your hair, I guess? Keep telling your joke."

"There's a spider in my HAIR?" Instantly I put my fingers in my hair and then stop. I don't really want to poke the spider. Aarghh! What am I supposed to do?

Hugo is trying not to laugh, but instead he just makes a fart sound with his lips. Oh, so he won't laugh when it's supposed to be funny, but he will when it's not? Great friend!

"Could be," Grandpa replies. Why does he not seem worried about this? "Anyway, Max, you were telling a joke."

"I can't finish my joke now! You need to come and check my hair!"

Good idea, Max. Make him fix this situation. The spider can bite his fingers.

"Right in the middle of your practice?"

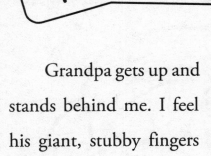

RIGHT NOW!!

Grandpa gets up and stands behind me. I feel his giant, stubby fingers going through my hair. He's shoving my whole head from side to side.

"Don't look now, Max, but I think you'll find your friend thinks this is quite funny," Grandpa whispers. "There is no spider. Just play along."

Wait, what? There's no spider? I look at Hugo. He's trying really hard not to laugh, but I can see in his eyes that this is funnier than any of my jokes. Oh, wow, this is how Tumbles does it! I'm going to try to fool Hugo and play along.

"Can you see it in there?" I ask, keeping the panic in my voice.

HMMM. NOT YET. THERE IS A CANDY CANE UP HERE THOUGH.

"A candy cane?"

"Yep."

Hugo grins. He knows we're pretending, of course, but weirdly, it still works. It's kind of like throwing a ball back and forth. Grandpa throws me a candy cane, and I have to catch it, play along, and throw it back.

"Oh, good," I reply. "I've been looking for that since last Christmas."

"I'd give it back to you," Grandpa says, "but the raccoon is eating it."

There's another ball for me to catch. I feel a bit quicker with it this time.

"You mean Sooty-Butt?" I say. Hugo cracks and laughs out loud. This is becoming quite fun. There's no script. Not even any actual jokes. We're just making this up as we go along.

"Sooty-Butt is the name of the raccoon?" Grandpa asks.

"Yeah. He's been missing since March."

"Well, hopefully Sooty-Butt ate the spider, because I can't find it," Grandpa says. "It could have crawled into your ear, I guess."

Time to go crazy.

"INTO MY EAR! IT'S GOING TO EAT MY BRAIN!" I grab at my ears, pulling and screaming. Out of the corner of my eye, I check to see if Hugo is laughing. He's laughing all right.

"I suppose it's possible," Grandpa says.

Time for me to throw a ball of my own and see if Grandpa can catch it.

I stop suddenly and tilt my head to one side. "No, I don't want one right now."

"What?" Grandpa looks confused.

Come on, old man. Show me what you've got.

"You just asked if I wanted a drink of water," I say to him. "I said no, I don't want one right now."

"I didn't ask if you wanted a drink of water."

"Of course you did," I argue. "I just heard you. And no, thank you, I don't need a massage either."

"What are you talking about? I'm not asking you about water and I certainly didn't offer a massage!"

"Well, if you didn't, Grandpa, then who did?" I ask. Then I see the twinkle in Grandpa's eyes. He gets it.

"Maybe it was …" he says slowly.

I gasp. "It couldn't be …"

Hugo chuckles as he realizes where this is going.

"You think the spider crawled into my ear and then offered me a glass of water and a massage?" I ask.

Grandpa nods. "It's a very kind spider, if you think about it. Maybe you should try talking back?"

I use a quizzical expression and say, "Um, thank you, spider. What's your name … spider?"

I pretend to listen to the spider talking in my head.

"Did he answer?" Grandpa asks.

I open my eyes wide with terror.

"What did he say, Max?"

I turn and look at Grandpa. "He said he can't talk right now." I stagger backward. "He said it's rude to talk while eating."

Then I put my hand to my chest and fall to the ground dead. End of show!

Hugo laughs and claps. Grandpa claps too.

And he's got a big smile on his face. Looking at him, I remember that I've always wanted to make Grandpa smile. Now I have.

"You've got the idea," he says, and winks at me. "You'll be fine tonight."

I never thought I'd say this, but I think I really like my grandpa! He's just like me!

"Why don't you do it with me?" I ask. "We could do the spider joke."

"That's a great idea," says Hugo. "We could sneak Tumbles in the back door and he could come out onstage halfway through your act."

THEN YOU CAN STILL DO YOUR BIG GRANDPA REVEAL AND YOU'LL HELP ME BE FUNNIER.

"You don't need my help, Max."

"I think I probably definitely do, Grandpa. Can you help me?"

"Yeah, he definitely needs your help," Hugo chimes in. Okay, buddy. Don't overdo it.

"Fine, fine," Grandpa says, and turns to his Tumbles costume.

ARE YOU UP FOR ONE LAST HURRAH, YOU OLD CLOWN?

26 It's my big night!

That evening, Mom, Dad, Rosie, Hugo, and I arrive at the town hall just as it's getting dark. I can't get over how many people are here. This must be the whole of Redhill!

Can I really make all these people laugh?

Maybe the only thing they'll be laughing at is me in this tuxedo. I look like a penguin! And this bow tie is very tight. Oh, well. You've got to look the part, I guess.

Big night. Little penguin!

I still can't believe Grandpa was Tumbles the whole time and that he was once a funny kid, just like me. He's always been such a cranky old man, but joking with him today, he was so different. He was fun. Making people laugh does that to you. It's like having soda and ice cream and jelly beans all in your mouth at the same time.

Maybe when Grandpa quit being Tumbles, he stopped being himself. That would probably make you pretty grumpy.

I look up at Mom and Dad. It's been a very big week. I'm excited that all the stress is about to be over for them. They're going to get to see Grandpa right in the middle of my act.

I say good-bye to Mom, Dad, and Rosie. They wish me luck and I run off after Hugo. He is going to smuggle Tumbles in through the backstage door once the show has started. Tumbles and I are the last act of the night.

Rupert is running around like a chipmunk on a sugar-only diet. He buzzes by me, turning only to say, "You better have something special, Max!"

"It's going to be good. Don't worry!"

For the first time this week, I'm actually not feeling nervous. Tumbles is the most popular act around and we're going to finish the whole show together. This is in the bag.

I stand in the wings with Hugo as the lights go down and the hall hushes.

The mayor says something we can't hear and then it's go time.

Abby is first. She does her disappearing magic trick perfectly and everyone loves it. Next is the saucepan man and he's followed by the opera singer, who sings so loudly that by the end of the song no one can hear anything anymore. That's not too big a deal, because the mime artist is next.

While he's doing his thing, Hugo nicks off to get Tumbles. No one seems to understand the guy dressed as a horse, but halfway through his act, Hugo comes back and taps me on the shoulder.

WE HAVE A PROBLEM ...
I CAN'T FIND TUMBLES.

WHAT?

I turn and grab Hugo by the shoulders. "What do you mean you can't find him?"

"He's not by the back door where we agreed to meet. I even ran over to the warehouse, but he's totally packed up and gone!"

I can't believe it! How could Grandpa do this? Doesn't he know that I can't do the spider act by myself? It doesn't work with one person. And every time I've done a stand-up comedy act alone, I've completely bombed.

THIS IS PAYBACK.

"What?"

"Karma or whatever they call it," I mutter. "When you do bad stuff and it comes back to bite you on the bum. Hugo, this is about to be a disaster."

"Max, look at me," Hugo says.

I turn and look at my life coach.

YOU'VE GOT THIS. YOU CAN DO IT. YOU DON'T NEED YOUR GRANDPA. YOU DON'T NEED TUMBLES. IT'S TIME TO AWAKEN THE ABOMINABLE SNOWMAN WITHIN YOU. YOU'RE MAX WALBURT. YOU ARE THE FUNNY KID. NOW IT'S TIME FOR THE REAL FUNNY KID TO PLEASE STAND UP!

He puts his hand in the air for a high five.

"You read my dad's book, didn't you?" I say.

"What was it your mom said?" Hugo's hand is still raised. He's going to be waiting awhile. "It's time to get up and knock down a horse."

Nope. Pretty sure that wasn't it.

"Thanks, Hugo."

Rupert grabs me by the arm and yanks me over to the curtains. Countdown has started.

Then they call my name.

My life is over.

27 Ooh. It's dark out here.

I walk slowly out into the middle of the stage.

The town hall is absolutely full of people and there's a huge round of applause as I move toward the spotlight and the microphone. I've never seen so many people in one place! I look down at my hands. They're shaking.

The room goes silent.

Without Tumbles, I actually have no idea what I'm going to say.

I cough a little to clear my throat. The microphone makes it so loud it sounds like there's a *T. rex* in the hall. Whoa.

It's dark out there, but I can just make out Mom, Dad, and Rosie. Right now I would much rather be sitting down there with them than standing up here.

But here I am. On my own. And everyone is waiting for me to say … something.

This is getting awkward.

Good start, Max. Good start.

"Has anyone seen my clown?"

I hear some awkward chuckling.

"Seriously. I have a clown who often pops up and boos me at inappropriate times. If you see him, can you do me a favor and hit him with a giant inflatable hammer?"

Some more chuckling. What did Grandpa say? Play a character. Characters in stories sometimes work better than jokes.

Which is good, because I, ah, didn't bring any jokes.

I continue. "He was supposed to be here today, but he called in sick. Apparently laughter isn't the best medicine after all."

That gets a laugh.

"Feel better?" I ask the audience. "Didn't think so."

Okay. That worked too. I keep going.

SPEAKING OF NOT BEING HERE, MY GRANDPA RAN AWAY FROM HOME THIS WEEK. WELL, THAT'S WHAT THE POLICE THOUGHT. I DIDN'T REALIZE GROWN-UPS RAN AWAY FROM HOME. I KNOW SOMETIMES KIDS DO. I RAN AWAY FROM HOME ONCE. I WAS TRYING TO FIND THE ICE-CREAM TRUCK PARKING LOT.

I look down at Mom and Dad. They're laughing because they remember it. It feels good to be able to make them laugh.

"Think about it," I say. "The ice-cream trucks have to park somewhere! Maybe it's the same place they keep the cotton-candy machines

and the hot-dog stands. When I grow up, that's where I want to work. I want to be the parking attendant at the Sugar Truck Parking Lot." More laughter. "It's important to have dreams."

People are actually really laughing, in that surprised, I-didn't-think-this-kid-would-be-funny

kind of way. This is awesome! All I'm doing is telling stories, just like Grandpa was doing, but I'm throwing the balls to myself, catching them, and throwing them back up into the air again. It's a bit like juggling, I guess.

"Maybe that's where my grandpa ran away to! Has anyone checked Sugar Truck Parking Lot? I bet that's where he is. Trying to cure his diabetes, one chocolate ice cream at a time."

Everyone seems relaxed now. I can't believe it. They're laughing and I don't even need to explain the jokes!

"It's an apple a day that keeps the doctor away, Grandpa. Not a caramel apple a day."

And that's when I look up to the back row of the town hall and there, standing in the doorway, is Grandpa – laughing!

What's he doing up there? Why is he not dressed as Tumbles? Why isn't he onstage with me?

Grandpa winks at me. It's almost as if he's saying I'm doing well.

And that's when I realize that he's done me a favor. I'm okay standing up here. Sure, I needed a little help to get here, but maybe sometimes all we need to do is ask for help.

Okay. I get it. I wink back at Grandpa. All right, then. Let's wrap this show up.

"You know what?" I say. "That must have been what happened to my clown. That's why he had to call in sick. Caramel apples! In that case, if you do see him, don't hit him with an inflatable hammer. Hit him with a banana or two instead, would you?"

The crowd stands and applauds!

28 And the winner is ...

I walk back off the stage. The curtains come down and the mayor tells everyone to talk among themselves while the judges decide who the winner is.

Hugo is jumping up and down and still trying to high-five me, but I peek through the curtains and watch as Grandpa slowly walks through the audience to where Mom, Dad, and Rosie are sitting.

They leap up and hug him. Then it looks like they get a bit angry with him and then hug him again. I think my mom is crying a bit. Rosie certainly is, but that might be because she just got her thumb stuck in her ear.

Grandpa points up to the stage and I can tell they're talking about me. He's smiling. It almost looks like he's proud of me. They all seem to be.

Maybe I might spend a bit more time at Redhill Nursing Home from now on. Grandpa can teach me how to keep getting better at being funny. Maybe we can make some of the other old people laugh and play pranks on Dr. Donkey-Butt. I can show him my mouse prank!

"Hey, Max?"

Abby's voice shatters my thoughts in the way that only she can. I turn around … and get a surprise. There's a girl standing next to Abby who I've never seen before.

"Nice job on your act and stuff," Abby says.

I don't really hear her though. I can't stop looking at the girl beside her. I don't know why … I just can't look … anywhere else. This is so weird.

The girl smiles at me.

"Hey! Max!" Hugo smacks me over the back of the head to get my attention.

Okay, easy, buddy.

"This is my friend Pip," Abby says as I rub my head. "She's starting at our school next week. She'll be coming to camp with us."

"We're going to camp?" I ask.

Abby turns to her friend. "Pip, this is Max Walburt. Everyone calls him the funny kid, but once you get to know him, you'll realize he's just a very rare species of idiot."

"Max, they're about to announce the winner!" Hugo calls out.

I turn away from Abby and Pip to join Hugo by the curtains, just as the mayor of Redhill finishes his speech.

"And the winner of tonight's Redhill's Got Talent is none other than ..."

I put my hand on Hugo's shoulder.

YOU KNOW, YOU'RE A PRETTY GOOD LIFE COACH, HUGO.

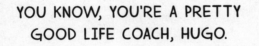

I THINK I'M GOING TO WRITE A BOOK.
THAT'S A GREAT IDEA. I THINK IT SHOULD BE MY LIFE STORY. HAVE I EVER TOLD YOU THAT I CAN REMEMBER BEING BORN?

Kids all over the world
are emailing Matt
their Funny Kid reviews!

Email him yours!

matt.stanton@gmail.com

Are you ready for Funny Kid #3?
Look out for
FUNNY KID: PRANK WARS!

This one is GREEN and it's full of pranks!

Have you read the very first
Funny Kid book?

FUNNY KID FOR PRESIDENT!

This one is BLUE
and someone poops in
the storeroom!

Thank you!

There are so many tremendous people who travel with me on my quest to make the funniest books for kids.

Beck, the person I spend every day with, is always first. This has been a huge year, stepping out boldly together to give this everything we have, and I wouldn't want to be doing it with anyone but you. Bonnie, Boston, and Bump, you put the colours in my day. I love you like a crazy person.

I've realised even more this last year how rare the encouragement and support my parents, Sue and Peter, and my sister, Hannah, have given me. Thank you.

I've worked in publishing houses, so I know how much effort, how many hours, how much sweat and stress and tears happen at my publishing house while someone else (me) takes all the credit. The team at HarperCollins Australia & New Zealand is exceptional.

Thank you firstly to my publisher, Chren Byng, to whom this book is dedicated. You wear so many hats for Beck and me, and I can't imagine this happening as it has without you. This book is for you.

To Kate Burnitt and Jeanmarie Morosin, who edited *Funny Kid Stand Up* – I rely on your eye for detail, so thank you for being so wonderful at what you do! To Michelle Weisz, Holly Frendo, Jacqui Barton, Kady Holt, Amy Fox, Darren Kelly, Gemene Heffernan-Smith, Bianca Carnevale, and Elizabeth O'Donnell – you all put in *so much* work getting Max's face in front of as many kids as possible and I find it so humbling that you would spend this much time working on something that just came out of my head.

To Cristina Cappelluto and James Kellow –
you two are incredibly smart, no matter what
anyone says. (Jokes!) Your wisdom carries
incredible weight for Beck and me, and the
HarperCollins Family really does feel like a family.
We look forward to taking this all the way.

Thank you, David Linker, my publisher in the
United States. You have really invested in Funny
Kid and for that I am incredibly appreciative.
Also to Meaghan Finnerty, Joe Merkel, Andrea
Vandergrift, and in the United Kingdom, Rachel
Denwood and Harriet Wilson, thank you!

Thank you, Kris Butson, for helping me see
as many students as I've been able to this past year!

Lastly to you, the 30,000+ kids and your
teachers whom I have had the joy of visiting so
far. I made this book for you. I hope it makes you
laugh. Keep reading!

Matt Stanton, 2017

Matt Stanton is a bestselling children's author and illustrator, with over a quarter of a million books sold. He is the cocreator of the megahits *There Is a Monster Under My Bed Who Farts* and *This Is a Ball*. His much anticipated middle-grade series, Funny Kid, launched around the world in 2017.

www.mattstanton.net

Come and subscribe to
Matt's YouTube Channel!

Matt Stanton's
**funny
drawing
show**

We learn to draw
funny stuff!

Talk about how to
write funny stories!

LIVE!

funny kid

Now, that's
what you call a
Book launch

YEP! WE SHOT IT OUT OF A CANNON!

And sometimes
we launch a book
out of a cannon!

MattStantonTV
www.youtube.com/mattstanton